BROKEN TRUST

A MEGAN SCOTT / MICHAEL ELLIOTT MYSTERY

SANDRA NIKOLAI

BROKEN TRUST

Copyright © 2017 by Sandra Nikolai

www.sandranikolai.com

This is a work of fiction. All names, characters, institutions, places, and events portrayed in this novel are either products of the author's imagination or are used fictitiously. Any resemblance to actual persons, living or dead, business establishments, events or locales is entirely coincidental.

All rights reserved, including the right to reproduce this book, or portions thereof, in any form or by any means.

Vemcort Publishing

ISBN: 978-1-989011-00-3 (eBook)

ISBN: 978-1-989011-02-7 (Paperback)

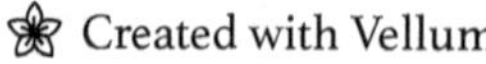 Created with Vellum

To our brave first responders.

1

The sluggish service at the front desk of the Dorfin Hotel was grating on my nerves.

Michael occasionally scanned his phone for messages and chatted with the person in line behind us. I couldn't pretend to be as composed. The A/C on our rental car had broken down soon after our departure from Montreal on one of the hottest July nights ever. All I wanted was a room with a shower after our two-hour drive to Ottawa.

It was nine o'clock and our turn to be served. Finally.

My hopes were dashed when a young clerk—Eric, his nameplate read—grew more flustered with every key he tapped on the computer.

"Long day?" Michael smiled at him.

Eric grimaced. "The computer's all weird." He glanced at Andy, an older clerk in a matching dark vest and bow tie, who was busy speaking with a customer. Eric turned back to the computer and hit a key. The transaction beeped through. With a toothy grin, he handed Michael his keycards. "Sorry for the delay. Enjoy your stay at the Dorfin Hotel." He offered us a pamphlet: Ottawa's 150th Anniversary Festivities.

Fat chance. This was no celebration trip. I stuffed the pamphlet into my handbag.

With luggage in tow, Michael and I took the elevator up. We plodded along the hallway to room 634, avoiding dinner plates stacked on trays in front of rooms, the leftovers emitting a concoction of smells from grilled hamburger to spicy sauces.

The Dorfin Hotel was only a ten-minute drive from downtown Ottawa, and we were lucky to have reserved a room a year ago. The city—Canada's capital—was now in party mode and all the hotels were fully booked.

Not that either of us had much time to party. We were here on business. Mostly.

Michael slid one of the keycards into the slot. The green LED blinked, and he opened the door for me.

I flicked on the overhead light, then sauntered along the narrow entrance into the room. A carafe of wine and two glasses sat on a table by the window. "Look, Michael. Room service left us some wine."

Something in the shadows to the right diverted my attention. A woman was sprawled motionless on the bed, her complexion pasty, her eyes glazed over!

I screamed, dropped my bag, and ran back toward Michael, almost knocking him over.

He grabbed me by the arms, steadying us. "Megan, what—"

"There's a woman on the bed." I trembled, struggling to catch my breath. "I think she's dead!"

He released his hold on me and pressed forward.

My stomach did flip-flops, but like a gawking witness at the scene of an accident, I couldn't avert my eyes. I took a step closer. The faint trace of the young woman's perfume lingered in the air, negating the fact that her heart had stopped beating.

Who was this woman?

How had she died?

And how did she get into our room?

Michael turned on the bedside lamp and stared at the body.

The woman had shoulder-length blonde hair and wore a revealing black lace teddy. Her makeup, though expertly done, failed to conceal the paleness of her skin or the blue tinge of her lips. Her mouth was partially open, as if she'd died before she could utter her last words.

Unnerved, I shifted my gaze to the contents that had spilled from a small purse beside her. A tube of lipstick, a driver's license, several business cards, and a plastic sleeve containing blue pills. A cell phone lay within inches of her outstretched hand. Her nails were painted red and white stripes—the colors of the Canadian flag. She wore a wedding band on her left hand.

Michael gently put his fingers on her wrist and confirmed our findings. "I'm not getting a pulse. Call the cops!"

I drew in a quick breath. My hands shook as I fumbled in my handbag for my phone.

This shocking turn of events was not on our agenda.

2

My heart pounded as the line rang.

The monotone voice of a female dispatcher came through. "911, what is your emergency?"

Her French-Canadian accent was apparent, so I relayed the details in French. When she asked for the hotel address, my mind went blank.

My eyes flitted about the room and fell on a complimentary notepad on a desk. I read off the address.

After the dispatcher confirmed the police were on their way, Michael contacted hotel management. "They're sending up a clerk," he said to me afterward. "I need to take some photos —fast."

"Why? It's not as if the police will think we had anything to do with this. She's obviously been dead for a while." I stole a peek at her. There was something surreal about being in the same room as a body whose essence had already left it. I fought a wave of nausea and focused on Michael instead. "Besides, it's none of our business."

It was completely our business, but I was reluctant to get involved. Such matters rarely turned out well for us.

"I'm all for taking precautionary measures." He aimed his phone at the woman and the objects on the bed and tapped away. He took photos of the wine carafe and two glasses on the table, the woman's clothes draped on the armchair in the corner, and her overnight bag.

I cast a wary eye toward the closed door. "Michael, the clerk is going to be here at any moment."

"No problem. I'll be quick." He took photos of the pills and the three business cards next to the woman's purse. "The names on some of these business cards read like governmental affiliations or agencies." His eyes widened. "What the hell?"

"What's the matter?"

"I recognize one of the names. Randall Thorne. He heads an external advisory group called Addiction Recovery Foundation. His national organization is based in Halifax, but he's working from his Ottawa office this week. I'm supposed to interview him on Monday."

"What about the names on the other cards?"

"Jerry Leduc from a company called Looking Ahead and another business card from a woman's clinic," Michael said. "I've never heard of either." He bent over to peer inside the woman's purse but didn't touch anything. "There's a lot of cash in here. A couple of other things at the bottom. Maybe keys." He used his zoom and took more photos.

"What about those pills? Do you think she overdosed?"

"Could be."

There was a knock at the door.

Michael slipped his phone in a side pocket of his cargo shorts.

I opened the door.

Eric stood there, fidgeting with his hands. "We received a call about a body. They sent me to see if... Well, sometimes we get hoax calls about stuff like this."

"I promise you, it's not a hoax." I invited him inside, then closed the door, leaving it ajar a few inches.

Eric crept up to the bed. "Oh, crap!" He put his hand to his mouth and raced to the bathroom, then bent over the toilet bowl.

I was already battling my own nausea. I shut the door to give Eric privacy and to block out the sound of his retching. "So much for not believing us," I whispered to Michael.

"Can't blame the poor kid," he said, keeping his voice low. "It's probably his first time seeing a corpse."

My most painful memory was a trip to the morgue to identify my late husband several years earlier. "Believe me, it doesn't get any easier."

Michael put a hand on my shoulder. "Sorry, Megan. I didn't mean to make light of it."

The door swung open and a broad-shouldered man in a dark blue jacket and jeans strode in, a police badge hanging from a lanyard around his thick neck. As he glimpsed Michael, his face lit up. "Michael Elliott. I thought I recognized the name on the dispatcher's report. You're the last person I expected to see here." He shook hands with him.

Michael introduced me to Detective Sergeant Ryan Grist of the Ottawa Major Crime Unit. I didn't mind his use of a new title—research assistant. It added flair to my otherwise boring label: ghostwriter of non-fiction documentation.

"Megan." The detective's eyes held my gaze as he firmly shook my hand, then he turned to Michael. "Are you covering this from an investigative reporter's angle, or did you just happen in on the scene here?" He glanced at the woman's body.

"We're visiting Ottawa," Michael said. "We checked in a few minutes ago and they gave us this room."

Detective Grist approached the bed and checked the woman's pulse. He retrieved his phone and contacted the police forensic ID unit with a request for services. Afterward, he asked us, "Do either of you know this woman?"

"I've never seen her before," Michael said.

"Me neither," I said.

"I supposed as much." The detective smiled wryly, then peered at the items on the bed. "Little blue pills. She might be a user." He motioned to the carafe of wine and two glasses on the table. "She was expecting someone to join her. The bed hasn't been slept in—or so it seems. Not surprising. A woman this beautiful doesn't usually drink or sleep alone." He looked at us. "Unless you guys ordered the wine for yourselves."

Was his compliment aimed at me or was he simply fishing for the truth?

"The wine was here when we arrived," Michael said.

The detective moved away from the bed and examined the wine glasses. "Lipstick. She probably took a sip or two." He returned to his former spot by the bed and examined the items that had spilled from the woman's purse. As Michael had done, he took photos of them with his phone, then peeked inside the purse without touching it. "Lots of cash in here. Some john probably paid her off." He tucked his phone away.

Resentment stirred inside me. "The dark blue two-piece suit on the chair is something a woman would wear to a corporate office, not on a street corner."

The detective straightened up. "I know how working girls like this one operate. The city's escort services cater to an active clientele in the bureaucratic segment. The clients book rooms at the Dorfin and other hotels on a regular basis. If their home-town is a considerable distance away, they keep their room tabs on a running bill as part of their lodging expenses. You can imagine how discreet the escorts have to be. That discretion extends to their appearance."

I refused to accept his assumption. "She's wearing a wedding ring."

Detective Grist shrugged. "It never stopped a woman from having an extra-marital affair."

My husband had had numerous affairs with other women

before he succumbed to an early death. Even though I didn't know how the woman in this room had died, I could relate to the sudden and unfortunate demise of one so young. And yet...

"It takes two to tango."

The detective frowned. "My point exactly."

Michael jumped in. "Megan's right. I'd want to know more about this woman before I jumped to any conclusions."

"I don't doubt your capabilities," the detective said. "You were damn thorough in that drug investigation we handled in Toronto a few years back. It saved me a load of legwork. I owe you one." He grinned. "Anyway, you should know me better by now. I work fast but analyze every piece of evidence before I draw my final conclusions." He surveyed the items on the bed again.

The flushing of the toilet broke the silence.

Detective Grist drew his gun and aimed it at the bathroom door.

I gasped.

Michael shouted, "No, it's okay!"

Our attention riveted on Eric as he exited the bathroom. He was pale, and his legs wobbled as if he were stepping on marshmallows. He caught sight of the detective's gun and raised his hands in the air.

"And who are you?" Detective Grist asked him.

"I'm—I'm Eric Tallow. I work at the front desk."

The detective put his gun away. "You can relax, Eric."

Eric lowered his hands and stared at the floor.

The detective dug out a pen and notebook. "You saw the body, Eric?" He motioned toward the bed.

Eric kept his eyes downcast. "Yes, sir."

The detective took a few steps toward him. "Do you realize you just contaminated a potential crime scene in there?" He gestured toward the bathroom.

"I couldn't help it. I was sick."

Detective Grist gestured toward the bed. "Have you seen this woman before today?"

Eric shook his head. "No, sir. I don't know what happened... how she got into this room. It was supposed to be empty."

"Maybe a mix-up in room numbers?"

"I'll go review the computer records at the front desk." He started to walk away.

"Wait," the detective called after him. "Let me know what you find. And stick around. I'll need to ask you more questions later."

"I'll be working at the front desk till midnight. Is there anything else you need, sir?"

"Yes," the detective said. "Get this nice couple another room for the rest of their stay here. Okay?"

"I'll go speak with Andy, my supervisor." Eric gave a nod in our direction, then hurried out, shutting the door behind him.

Detective Grist flipped to a new page in his notebook. "Michael, tell me what time you arrived here, what you saw... You know the drill."

Michael filled him in, including his call to the front desk.

The detective scribbled notes. "Did either of you touch the body or anything else in the room?"

"I took the woman's pulse." Michael surveyed the room. "I turned on the lamp by the bed."

"We touched the door handles...and the door," I said. "I touched the light switch in the entrance."

"We might need to take your fingerprints to eliminate yours should this turn out to be a crime scene," the detective said. "How long will you be in town?"

"A week," Michael said.

"I'll keep in touch." Detective Grist put away his pen and notebook. "I've posted a uniform outside the door. Forensics are on their way." He glanced at the body again. "What a waste. Those pills could have done her in. If this is a drug overdose—

heroin, morphine, or whatever—it's just the latest addition to the opioid abuse cases exploding across the country."

"Don't I know it," Michael said. "I've been researching the topic. The Public Health Agency of Canada reported several thousand deaths last year from opioid-related overdoses. Ottawa isn't exempt from the same crisis."

The detective nodded in agreement. "It's hitting the city big time. We can barely keep up with the number of fatalities caused by the illicit trade of fentanyl-laced drugs."

"Drug traffickers lace their counterfeit pills with fentanyl because it's a hundred times more potent than morphine and about fifty times stronger than heroin. Unsuspecting users don't know what they're buying."

"Until it's too late." The detective paused. "So what brings you two to Ottawa?" His eyes lingered on me.

"I'm working on a project covering the city's festivities for Canada's 150th anniversary," I said.

The detective smiled. "Sounds like you're going to have fun."

"It's still work." I hated having to justify my efforts. "I'm also assisting Michael with his research."

He switched his focus to Michael. "Research? On what?"

"It's an investigative piece for *The Gazette* in Montreal," he said. "The topic is the abuse of and addiction to opioids, with the information on pain medication like fentanyl. I'm meeting with the addiction authorities this week to find out what steps they've taken to control the drug abuse crisis and help addicts."

"A timely topic," the detective said. "I attended two national conventions on fentanyl drug abuse this month. The police, public health, fire, and paramedic—we're all involved. The local epidemic of counterfeit pills that contain fentanyl has spread from back alleys to the suburbs. From young teens over-dosing at drug parties to middle-class adults who died from ingesting a single pill."

"Do you think this latest victim fits into the last category?"

The detective gestured toward the woman on the bed. "This looks like a suicide or an accidental overdose to me, but I can't be sure until the autopsy results come in. If you hear anything from other hotel guests that might prove helpful, let me know." He exchanged business cards with Michael. "In the meantime, try to enjoy some of the events while you're here."

Michael and I said our goodbyes, then grabbed our luggage and left.

I waited until we'd moved a distance from the uniformed officer standing outside our abandoned room 634. "Sounds like you know Detective Grist well," I said to Michael.

"We worked together to bring down a drug trafficking ring in Toronto," he said. "Grist gave me permission to ride along on a couple of their drug busts."

"Oh. I see."

"What?"

"I don't know him as well as you do, and I could be wrong, but I think he's reckless in his assumptions. He has no proof, yet he's already hinting the woman could have killed herself. And did you see how fast he drew his gun? Poor Eric."

"He didn't know the kid was in there. Anyway, Grist is a good investigator."

"He probably has a backup team to help him."

Michael grinned. "Yeah. He sure loves to delegate."

"Is that what he meant about you doing all the legwork in that Toronto case?"

"You got it."

I was curious. "What exactly did you do for him?"

"I met with drug dealers and informants on the street."

"Uh-huh. Why do I get the impression he wouldn't hesitate to drag you into another dangerous situation if it came up?"

"Only if I agree to it." Michael checked his watch. "I hope the hotel has another room available for us."

"Are you deliberately changing the subject?"

He chuckled. "You worry too much about me."

"With good reason. You thrive on risky business."

"You can relax, Megan. I have no intention of jumping into any covert investigative assignments while we're here."

"You say that every time."

He put his arm around me. "I mean it this time."

"What about the name on the business card you recognized back there?"

"Right." Michael grew pensive. "I'll discreetly ask Randall Thorne about it on Monday."

"Why not let the police handle it? I'm sure they're going to interview him."

He remained silent.

"Oh, I get it," I said. "You just can't let it go, right? You have to get involved."

His brow furrowed. "We're already involved. We walked right into a crime scene. It's destiny."

"But we had nothing to do with her death."

"I want to know how she died."

We cut short our conversation as we approached three people standing by the elevator.

A gray-haired woman was saying, "The police are still investigating. I'm telling you, something very strange happened in that room over there." She motioned toward the hallway.

Not one to miss an opportunity, Michael edged into their conversation. "Excuse me. I couldn't help overhearing. Are you referring to a room on this floor?"

The elderly woman looked up at him. "Yes, I am. Room 634 —the room adjacent to mine." She gestured toward the hallway again. "It's the room with the police officer standing in front of it."

"We noticed him too," Michael said, playing along. "Do you know what happened?"

"Whatever it is, it can't be good. Minutes ago, a clerk came out of there and rushed down the hallway to the elevators. He looked as if he'd seen a ghost."

A balding man in a white polo shirt chimed in. "If you ask me, there's something fishy going on here. I paid good money to stay at this hotel, and I expect a certain level of security. I can't have a stranger rough up Evelyn for no reason." He placed a protective arm around the elderly woman, presumably his wife. "I've got a mind to tell the police about it."

"No, Wally," Evelyn said. "I don't want to cause any trouble."

"What happened?" I asked her.

She sighed. "A man bumped into me hard as I was leaving my room this afternoon. My shoulder still hurts." She put a hand over it. "He didn't even stop to apologize. So rude."

"Sounds like he was in a hurry," Michael said.

"He was probably going to one of the late day sports events in town," Evelyn said. "He was certainly dressed for it."

"How?"

"A baseball cap, a T-shirt, and sunglasses."

"You might expect behavior like that from young people these days—not from a grown man," Wally said. "If I'd been there, I'd have told him a thing or two."

"You should have waited another ten minutes for me before going down," Evelyn said to him.

"I wanted to reserve a place in line for the five-thirty buffet," Wally explained for our benefit. "Good thing I got there fifteen minutes early. The line was getting long."

"Oh, well then." Evelyn huffed, then addressed Michael and me. "Standoffish guests order their meals through room service. Wally and I prefer to socialize at dinnertime. It's so nice to meet people from different places." She smiled. "Anyway, I'm not the only one who noticed weird goings-on here." She motioned to the other man in their group who hadn't said a word so far. "Tell them what you saw, Roger."

"I saw a young woman outside room 634." Roger's dark eyes protruded beneath messy hair and bushy eyebrows. "She seemed real strange. I didn't think much about it until a uniformed police officer turned up here tonight."

"What time was it you noticed her?" Michael asked him.

"It must have been about quarter to six. I'd just shaved for dinner." Roger passed a hand over his chin.

"Can you describe her?"

"She was quite the looker." Roger licked his lips. "Blonde hair down to her shoulders, well dressed. You just can't help noticing someone like that." He beamed, as if reliving the moment. "Yet there was something strange about her."

"Like what?" I asked him.

"She wore dark sunglasses and looked down as I came closer—like she didn't want anyone to notice her."

"What's so strange about that?"

"I'm not done," Roger said. "She knocked at the door, then fished for something in her purse. I didn't hang around to see if someone on the other side opened the door for her. When I got to my room, I turned around and she was gone. It was all so mysterious."

"She probably let herself in," Michael said. "Guests usually have keycards to their rooms."

"Guests don't knock on their own hotel door," I said.

"Hey, don't get me wrong." Roger held up his hands, palms outward. "I'm not a frigging stalker or anything." His boisterous laugh drew stares from passersby. "Like you said, maybe she let herself in. I don't know."

"I think you should stop by room 634 and tell the officer what you saw," Michael said to the threesome.

"I agree," I said. "It could be helpful."

"Helpful for what?" Evelyn asked.

"For whatever the police are investigating in room 634," Michael said.

"I think I'll do that right now." Roger took a few steps, then stopped and walked back to us. "By the way, what room are you guys in?"

"None," I said hastily. "There was a mix-up in our rooms." I stretched my arm to access the elevator button and prayed for a quick getaway.

"How unfortunate," Evelyn said. "What happened?"

"Uh...the one they gave us was already occupied."

The elevator doors opened.

"Bye. Gotta go." I nudged Michael toward the waiting car and waved goodbye to three gawking faces as the doors closed.

Some things you just have to keep to yourself.

3

———

Michael and I had a clear path to the front desk. True to his word, Eric was at his post. Andy was on the phone steps away from him, and a frown rippled across his forehead when he noticed us approaching.

As Eric greeted us with a smile, the whiff of peppermint wafted our way. "I'm so sorry about what happened. I just reviewed the computer records. I gave you the keycards to Room 634 instead of 643."

Michael shrugged. "Anyone can make a mistake like that."

Eric lowered his voice. "This job is the first full-time one I've ever held. I've only been working here a couple of weeks. It's been crazy with all the tourists visiting the city." He hesitated. "I want to make a good impression on my boss, so please don't lodge a complaint against me." His eyes searched our faces.

A pang of guilt swept through me as I recalled how difficult my first real job had been as a bank cashier handling oodles of money. Talk about the jitters!

"We have nothing to complain about," Michael said.

"That's right," I said. "You were serving a lot of people at the front desk. Mistakes happen."

"Thanks." Eric relaxed somewhat. "As far as Room 634 goes, it was a double error."

"What do you mean?" I asked.

He kept his voice low. "Housekeeping had done up the room because the regular occupant—some fat-cat bigwig—told us he'd be gone for the weekend. I shouldn't have allocated that room to anyone else. On top of that, I fudged the room numbers. I was supposed to give you room 643 to begin with."

"Let me get this straight," I said. "No one was supposed to be in that room this weekend?"

"That's right," Eric said. "Please, keep this between us."

"So how did the woman get in?"

"I haven't a clue." He grimaced, as if he were replaying his horrifying visit to the room.

Andy completed his call and sauntered over. He greeted Michael and me, subtly nudging Eric and forcing him to step aside.

Eric blushed and slowly slid away to another monitor.

"Management deeply regrets any inconvenience that you might have experienced," Andy said to us. "As a token of our customer appreciation, we would like to offer you a penthouse suite during your stay here. Fully paid." He held out two gold keycards.

"That's not necessary," Michael said, stopping short of accepting the cards.

"We insist." Andy held his chin up and his shoulders back. "It's the least we can do under the circumstances."

"Okay. Thanks." Michael accepted the cards and put them in his pocket. He glanced around, making sure no one was within hearing range. "By the way, Andy, do you have a few moments? I'd like to talk to you."

Michael caught me by surprise. Sometimes his actions were unpredictable. The upside was that they were based on investigative instincts that I'd come to admire.

"Sure," Andy said. "How can I help you?"

"We booked our room here a year ago," Michael said. "It was impossible to find a vacancy in the hotels closer to the city core. Since Ottawa is a government town, I was wondering if government employees have first dibs on rooms here."

"Not necessarily," Andy said. "When major events occur in the city, the rooms available to the general public are reserved long in advance. It's probably why you had a hard time booking a room."

"Makes sense."

I couldn't leave without probing further. "By the way, we understand there was a mix-up in our rooms."

Andy gave me a practiced smile. "Yes, a technical glitch of sorts. Again, we sincerely apologize for the mistake. Can I help you with anything else?"

"No," Michael said. "Thanks."

"Enjoy your stay at the Dorfin Hotel." Andy forced another smile.

On the way to the elevator, Michael whispered to me, "The penthouse suite. Talk about a bribe."

"Management wants us to stay quiet," I said.

"Sure looks like it. Eric said the regular occupant of room 634 was some fat-cat bigwig. I bet he works for the government or big business. I need to find out who he is."

He aroused my curiosity. "How can we do that?"

"We?" Michael grinned.

"Yes. Why not?"

"You didn't sound too interested a while ago."

"I admit I'm still reeling from what happened, and I don't think I'll ever forget it. That's beside the point. Who wouldn't want to know how a young woman ended up dead in their hotel room?"

"Right."

"And don't we always work better as a team?"

"Right again."

"About the occupant of that room... You were saying?"

Michael lowered his voice. "I'll contact my tech buddy in Montreal tonight. He's a whiz who can hack into elaborate computer systems. He'll tell us who had access to that room within a specific time frame."

"That's illegal, Michael. And unethical."

He shook his head so-so. "Not exactly. He's a certified ethical hacker and a white hat."

"What does that mean?"

"He doesn't break into secure networks to destroy data for malicious reasons or steal information to commit crimes for personal gain. He uses his abilities for good, ethical, and legal purposes. In this case, I happen to believe the end—finding a cold-blooded murderer, if it comes to that—justifies the means."

"What if your friend gets caught?"

"Don't worry. He's a pro. If anyone knows how to cover his tracks, he does."

4

———————

Coffee cup in hand, I joined Michael on the u-shaped sofa in our penthouse suite. We'd had breakfast delivered to our room Saturday morning—standoffish guests, as Evelyn would have labeled us. In truth, we didn't want to miss the news coverage on the big screen TV.

The report about a woman's demise at the Dorfin Hotel topped the Ottawa broadcast. She had now been identified as thirty-five-year-old Becca Landry who lived with her husband Frank and their two young children in the suburbs.

The news switched to live coverage. Reporters were interviewing Frank on the front porch of his two-story house. He was tall with short-cropped hair and beefy arms. Beside him stood his children and a gray-haired woman with the same round face and sharp eyes as Frank. She had to be his mother.

"I don't give a damn what the cops say," Frank said to reporters, his eyes blazing with anger. "Someone killed my wife, and I'm going to find out who it is if it's the last thing I do." His expression resolute, he refused to answer any more questions. He turned his back on the reporters and ushered his family into the house. The address plaque number 137 nailed to the siding vibrated when he slammed the door behind him.

The reporter on the scene ended the coverage by stating that police investigators did not suspect foul play and that autopsy results were expected soon.

I clicked off the TV. "How sad is that? Those kids can't be more than three or four years old, and now they have no mother. It's hard to believe that Becca Landry was a drug user. It doesn't make sense."

Michael raised an eyebrow. "You'd be surprised. The rising drug epidemic is knocking down assumptions about users. Grist confirmed as much too."

I resisted the notion of Grist's infallibility. "He could be wrong about Becca."

"We'll find out soon enough."

"Even if Becca was using, Frank is taking a chance to say she was murdered. I'm sure the police can't be too happy about that comment on live TV."

"He comes across as a guy who speaks his mind. I'd bet he doesn't care what anyone thinks. Regardless, the cops will work around it. Their spokesperson will portray Frank as a distraught and grieving husband looking for someone to blame for his wife's death."

"Do you think Frank knows something we don't?"

"Maybe. We'll find out once we interview him."

"Interview him? How? We don't even know where he lives."

Michael reached for his phone. "He might be listed in the online directory." After several tries, he said, "Nope. Nothing under Frank, Rebecca or Becca Landry, or their initials. It must be an unlisted number."

I crossed the floor to a small desk along the wall and opened the drawer. It held an alternative source of information: a phone directory from three years earlier. It was worth a search. Maybe Frank's phone number was publicly listed back then.

I returned to the sofa and scanned the white pages under *L* until I found a listing for Frank Landry. "Here it is. Take down this address and phone number."

Michael gave me a questioning look. "How do you know it's the right one?"

"The news coverage showed the address plaque on Frank's house. It was 137. There can't be too many people named Landry living at 137 whatever street."

"Good point."

While Michael recorded the details in his phone contacts, I flipped to the directory's business listings in the yellow pages. Detective Grist had mentioned there was a high demand for escort services in the city, so finding hundreds of names listed under Adult Entertainment shouldn't have surprised me. But it did.

"Let's drive directly to Frank's home," Michael said. "I don't want to ruin our chances of seeing him by calling him first."

"The surprise element," I said. "It sounds good, but he might still refuse to talk to us—especially after you introduce yourself as an investigative reporter."

"I can't lie to the guy."

I gave it some thought. "Then let's tell him the truth—that we were the ones who found his wife's body. We'll extend our condolences to him. If he's looking for answers, he might have questions."

Michael smiled. "You see? That's what I love about you. Your wit." He leaned over to kiss me.

"My wit? That's all?" I teased him.

He snuggled closer and put his arm around me. "I love your cooking too." He kissed me again.

"Good try, but you do most of the cooking at home."

"I love everything about you, Megan." He placed a lingering kiss on my lips that set off the butterflies in my stomach.

"Okay, you made your point." I laughed and wiggled out of

his embrace. "If we want to visit Frank Landry, we need to get going."

"Right." Michael stood up. "By the way, I've been going over the photos I took of the items in the hotel room. There are so many unanswered questions about the business cards, the load of cash in Becca's purse, the fentanyl pills..."

"I'm curious about the carafe of wine and the two glasses. Who was she expecting to join her?"

"If anyone can answer that question, it's her husband."

5

F rank Landry lived in Orleans, one of the many Ottawa suburbs that seemed to have developed overnight. Although such communities blossomed into mini cities, common interests and family values kept the residents integrated—especially through difficult times.

The pots of white calla lilies lining the porch of Frank's home negated the impression that the family had experienced a loss, but the memorial of teddy bears and flowers around the tall maple tree on the front lawn indicated the community was grieving along with them.

Despite my willingness to accompany Michael to Frank's home, I wasn't looking forward to our visit. We were arriving unannounced, and I wasn't a fan of the habit—not even with family and friends. I always called first. And if Frank's interview with reporters was any indication of the mood he was in, our impromptu visit wouldn't go over too well.

As Michael rang the bell at 137 Waterfall Crescent, my heart raced. I took a deep breath to quell my nerves.

The front door opened a crack. A fair-haired boy peeked out at us. He couldn't have been more than four years old.

From behind him came a woman's voice. "Cory, I told you to wait for Granny." A woman wearing a white apron gently nudged the boy aside and stood in the entrance, one hand on the partially opened door, the other holding a little girl's hand. The child was younger than her brother and had the same light-colored hair.

I recognized the grandmother from this morning's TV broadcast. "Hello. Is Frank Landry home?"

"I'm sorry. We're not answering any more questions from reporters." She started to close the door.

"Wait. I'm not a reporter." I raised my hands. "See. No cameras, no microphones."

The skepticism in her eyes was hard to miss. She glanced past us to the street where camera crews had set up shop earlier this morning but had since left to cover the next big story. "Who are you then?"

"I'm Megan Scott. This is Michael Elliott. We're staying at the Dorfin hotel. We called the police after we discovered Becca Landry dead in our hotel room." My words suddenly sounded so sterile. I could have kicked myself for not having thought of a more considerate way to put it. "We'd like to speak with Mr. Landry. Please."

She hesitated, lines scrunching up her face as she weighed the outcome of her decision. "Come on in." She shut the door behind us, then said to the children, "Cory, Olivia. Go fetch your daddy. Tell him we have visitors."

The children scrambled upstairs, calling after their father.

As Michael and I waited, the aroma of cookies fresh from the oven drifted our way. Our arrival had perhaps interrupted the grandmother's baking, but she'd invited us in regardless. I hoped Frank would be just as welcoming.

There was a scuffle of feet upstairs and moments later, the two children scampered back down.

Frank Landry followed, placing a hand on the railing as he descended, one step at a time, his journey hampered by a distinctive limp. A snug T-shirt over a pair of jeans revealed a fit, brawny torso. His dark hair was cut short, military style. As he reached the landing, he gave his mother a quizzical look.

She spoke in a quiet voice. "These folks are staying at the Dorfin Hotel. They called the police after they discovered Becca in their room. They would like to talk to you." To the children, she said, "Come with Granny. It's time for milk and chocolate chip cookies." She steered them across the foyer to the kitchen.

Michael and I introduced ourselves to Frank and offered our condolences.

"The police mentioned something about a mix-up with the hotel rooms and a call they received from guests who had found Becca," Frank said. "So that was you?"

"Yes," Michael said. "They assigned us the wrong room number. We walked in and found your wife collapsed on the bed. Then we called 911."

"By the time the police called me," Frank said, "Becca had already been transferred to the morgue. They asked me to go there to officially identify her. She looked so peaceful." His bottom lip quivered. "They haven't told me much. They don't even know how she died."

"They'll perform an autopsy to determine the cause of death."

"Yes. The detective mentioned they would." Frank gazed down for a moment. "Becca went through a rough patch the last while. Working long days. Even weekends sometimes. The kids and me, we don't get to see her much."

He almost made it sound as if Becca were still alive.

Frank continued. "My mom lives with us. She helps out with the kids and keeps order in the place." He glanced over his shoulder toward the kitchen. "I'd like to ask you some questions, if you don't mind. Why don't we sit down?" He steered us to the left of the foyer and into the living room.

Michael and I settled on a cushy fabric couch bordering a coffee table topped with a selection of paperback novels. Frank slowly eased himself into a matching armchair adjacent to us and stretched out his right leg.

On a corner table sat a framed photo of Frank and Becca taken on their wedding day. Another photo showed them with their two children, each of them sporting a baseball cap. A third frame displayed a photo of Frank with another man. Both men were dressed in military gear.

Michael pointed to the military photo. "Is this recent?"

"It was taken a couple of years ago," Frank said, smiling briefly. "Nino was a close friend." He took in a deep breath. "I returned from a tour of duty seven months ago that got cut short. Afghanistan." He rubbed his palm along his right thigh, almost caressing it.

"What happened?"

"We were military engineers and had to ensure the safety of the route for our armored vehicles. An IED exploded on a road we were patrolling. Shrapnel hit us. I injured my leg, but I survived. Nino wasn't so lucky."

Yet another loss. "So sorry to hear that," I said.

He shrugged. "Those are the risks you accept to take when you join the military. Now I can't get a damn job."

Michael guided the conversation back on track. "You said you had questions about Becca."

"Becca and I…" Frank sighed. "Like I said before, she'd been working long hours, so we rarely had time to be alone."

"What kind of work did she do?" I asked Frank.

"She was an administrator for a non-profit organization. They offer learning courses to help rehabilitate addicts. It's called Looking Ahead."

The name on one of the business cards in Becca's purse!

Beside me, Michael shifted a little but said nothing.

Frank heaved another sigh. "You have no idea how eager I was to spend the weekend with her."

"You had plans for the weekend?" I asked him. "At the Dorfin Hotel?"

Frank nodded. "Yesterday afternoon, Becca called me at home." He stopped. "Oh God, was it only yesterday? It's so hard to believe she's gone." He blinked back tears. "She asked if my mom could take care of the kids this weekend. She said she'd booked a room at the hotel for us and that I should pack a bag for a weekend stay. We hadn't spent much time together the last while, so I thought this would be the perfect way to revive our marriage." He paused in thought. "She told me she wanted to talk to me about something important but didn't have time to get into it on the phone. She said she'd meet me in the hotel lobby at six o'clock."

Relief flowed through me. Becca hadn't met some john as Detective Grist had implied. Yet something nagged at me. "Why didn't she give you the room number?"

"She said she didn't know the room number. She had to register at the front desk first."

"Did you go to meet her in the lobby then?"

"Yes," Frank said. "I got to the lobby, but she wasn't there. I waited fifteen minutes, then I called her cell phone. There was no answer. I left a message. I thought maybe she'd been delayed at work."

"Did you try to reach her there?"

"Yes, but there was no answer. I left a message anyway."

"Did you leave the hotel at that point?"

"No," Frank said. "I spoke to someone at the front desk and explained the situation. I wanted to know if Becca had booked a room in her name. I asked them to check their records, but they refused. They said it was against hotel policy...that they had to ensure the privacy of their guests."

"Did you show them ID to prove you were her husband?" Michael asked him.

"Yes, but it made no difference. They still refused."

"You must have been worried," Michael said. "What did you do then?"

Frank squeezed his lips. "I got angry. I decided to take off before I got real mad and punched someone out. I thought maybe Becca had gone home or something." He shook his head in frustration. "But when I got home, Becca wasn't here. I tried to reach her again. Now I know why she didn't answer my calls. She must have been dead by then."

Silence hung heavy in the air.

"If it can give you any consolation, a cell phone was on the bed next to Becca," I said. "She might have been reaching for it. She was trying to answer a call or wanting to call someone."

"Was she..." He chewed on his bottom lip. "Was she alone in the bed?"

His question—and the unexpectedness with which he introduced it—stunned me.

Michael remained unruffled. "Yes," he said in a quiet voice. "She was alone."

Frank focused on a spot on the carpeted floor as if he were trying to word the next question. "Was there any sign that...she might not have been alone earlier?"

"As far as we could tell, the bed hadn't been slept in," Michael said. "There was no sign that anyone else had been there except to deliver the wine."

"Wine?"

"Yes, a carafe of red wine and two glasses. The hotel staff probably delivered the wine before or after Becca got there."

Frank raised his voice. "It's impossible. She would never have ordered wine for us."

"Why not?"

"Becca and my mother had a glass of red wine but only on special occasions like Christmas. We never stocked up on wine or liquor at home though. It's off limits for me because I take painkillers. Fentanyl. It's the only thing that helps with the pain in my leg."

Michael picked up on the cue. "There was a small packet of pills on the bed next to Becca's purse."

Confusion washed over Frank's face. "What?"

"Was Becca using drugs?"

"Hell, no!" Frank stared at us. "Is that what you're thinking? That she was an addict?"

"The pills were blue," Michael said.

Frank's eyes widened. "Oh." He hung his head low. "They were probably mine."

"Yours?"

He nodded. "The fentanyl dosage the doctor prescribes for me is too low. The pain keeps me awake at night. Becca has a contact for the extra fentanyl pills I need. At a much cheaper price too."

"That's illegal. And risky. You can't be sure what's in them."

"Illegal or not, I can't live without them. I've been getting them from the same source for months, and I'm still here."

Michael pursued his line of questioning. "Do you know if Becca purchased the pills recently?"

"Probably on Friday. I was running short. She said she'd get a supply that same day."

"And you're sure she wasn't using?"

Frank stiffened. "Look, she definitely wasn't using, okay? I'm her husband. I should know."

We'd touched a nerve. Did Frank really know his wife, or was he pretending he did just to protect her?

I spoke softly. "Frank, your wife's death is a mystery right now. If you don't share what you know with the police, you'll never find out what happened."

"Look, I'm grateful for the information you've told me about Becca," Frank said. "In return, I owe you the truth. That's what I've given you." His tone mellowed. "We've had our problems, but Becca wasn't depressed or anything like that. You don't know her. She cheered everyone up the moment she walked through the door. She would never do herself in."

"We never suggested she did," Michael said.

"No, but that damn cop keeps asking me about it. What's his name?"

"Detective Ryan Grist," I said.

"Yeah, Grist," Frank said through his teeth. "If you ask me, he seemed to be in a rush to get on with it and close the file."

So I wasn't the only one who thought Grist's investigative process was hurried.

Michael went on. "In the TV newscast this morning, you told reporters you thought Becca was murdered."

Frank scowled. "I still do. The autopsy results will prove it. In the meantime, I'm going to find out who killed Becca. I promise you."

The determination in his eyes scared me. Considering his military training, I didn't doubt his capacity to follow through on his promise.

As if he'd read my mind, Michael asked him, "Why not let the police handle it?"

Frank clenched his fists. "Because I don't trust them to do the right thing."

"Why not?"

"They'll try to pin her murder on me. The spouse is always the most likely suspect."

My breath caught in my throat, and I coughed to cover it up.

Michael gave me a side-glance. He was no doubt recalling—as I was—how easily we'd become prime suspects in my husband's death years earlier.

Frank rubbed his leg. "Sorry about getting so personal. I can't help thinking that, if the cops are looking for someone to blame for Becca's death, I'd better get hustling and prove my innocence."

Michael leaned forward. "I'd like to help you find out what happened to Becca. It's time for me to be upfront with you now." He pulled out a business card and handed it to Frank. "I'm an investigative journalist. I promise you that everything we discussed here will remain confidential."

Frank tossed the card across the coffee table and grasped the armrests. "You've got a lot of nerve to come—"

Michael raised his hands, palms outward. "I promise you, I'm not here to get a story. I just want to help you."

Frank glared at him. "Help me? What makes you think I need your help?" He pushed himself out of the armchair and pointed to the front door. "Get out of my house! Now!"

6

———

W hat if Frank makes good on his threat and kills someone?" I asked Michael after we'd driven off.

"Let's hope logic kicks in before he regrets his actions." He steered the car onto the westbound Queensway. "He's walking a tightrope of emotions."

"I don't like the way his moods shift from depression to anger. It's scary. Then again, the recent loss of his wife could explain the fluctuations."

Michael pressed on the gas and switched into the passing lane. "A gut feeling tells me the increased fentanyl usage is affecting his emotions too."

"What's he supposed to do? He needs painkillers. Maybe he can't sleep without them."

"It's a catch-22, isn't it?"

"That's a given." My mind took off on a tangent. "I've been thinking about the questions Frank asked us. It sounds as if he suspected Becca was having an affair."

"Yeah. He stopped short of admitting as much."

"If they hardly saw each other, maybe their marriage was

suffering. One thing led to another, and the bond of trust between them broke."

"Which could have led to something else," Michael said.

"What are you getting at?"

"Becca was wearing a black lace teddy. She wasn't planning to go down to the lobby to meet Frank dressed like that, right?"

"She might have changed her mind about meeting him in the lobby. Maybe she wanted to call him and ask him to come up to the hotel room instead, but she never got the chance to follow through with her plan."

"I'm not sure about that."

"What are you insinuating?"

Michael pressed his lips together. "What if Frank's hunch was right? What if Becca invited someone else to the hotel earlier that afternoon? What if she didn't have time to get dressed before she met Frank in the lobby?"

"Impossible," I said. "The bed in the hotel room was neat and tidy."

"I'm sure she knew how to make a bed."

"You're beginning to sound like Frank. Or worse. Like Detective Grist."

"Thanks a lot."

"Let's be realistic. Becca was probably reaching for her phone to call Frank or return one of his calls to her. Something —or someone—prevented her."

"Grist thinks she did herself in."

"Absolutely not. Did you see those kids? What mother would leave her young children behind simply because her marriage was in trouble? I know I couldn't."

"That's good to know." Michael's blue eyes twinkled. "On both counts."

I sensed where the discussion was heading. "It doesn't mean I want kids—now or in the future. I'm only saying that if I had them, I'd take care of them, no matter how bad things got."

He smiled at me. "I'm sure you'd make a fine mother."

"Thanks." I guided the conversation back to our original topic. "About Becca, all I see is a woman who booked a relaxing weekend with her husband to try to salvage their marriage before it was too late. I can't believe she took the time to make those arrangements and then killed herself. Or that she'd make those arrangements with her husband, only to have a liaison right before."

"If you're right and it wasn't suicide, or an affair, it means someone wanted to get rid of her. What I'd like to know is who and why."

~

On our return to the penthouse suite, I sunk into the bulky sofa in the living room and tucked my feet under me. The day was half over and I was already exhausted.

Michael joined me and set his laptop on the coffee table. "Time to check out those business cards in the photos I took." He uploaded them from his phone to the laptop.

First up was Randall Thorne, head of Addiction Recovery Foundation. His photo on the website revealed a thickset, distinguished-looking man in his late fifties with a confident air that said, "Don't mess with me."

"Classy suit and expensive tie," I said. "Your typical high-ranking bureaucrat."

Michael grinned. "You can bet his suits don't come off the rack."

I scanned the information on the screen. Part of the group's mandate was to educate the public about substance abuse. "Interesting. About educating the public, I mean."

"It claims one of Thorne's sponsors is the Public Health Agency of Canada. Looks like his foundation distributes the big bucks to groups that offer courses to drug addicts wanting to turn their lives around."

"Timely. Who's up next in your business cards?"

"Jerry Leduc of Looking Ahead."

"Where Becca worked."

Michael typed the name and followed the link to a website.

The home page of Looking Ahead displayed a photo of Jerry Leduc, president of the organization. The forty-something man posed stiffly for the camera, his neck straining against a shirt collar that was too tight, his longish dark hair combed back and slicked down with gel.

Michael peered at the screen. "It's a non-profit organization. They must depend on financial handouts through government agencies and organizations, and public donations. They offer learning courses to candidates who want to get into the job market."

"Sounds promising," I said.

He nodded. "Some people lose their jobs, their homes, their families... They hit rock bottom and turn to drugs. They need help to put their lives back together again."

I leaned forward. "Click on that red button to see what kind of courses they offer."

Michael clicked on it. Another window opened, displaying a list of programs from A to W.

"Lots of choices." I noticed another detail on the screen. "What's that button? It says *code*."

He clicked on it. A small window opened up, asking for a code. "Must be for approved applicants only." He sat back. "I'd like to interview Jerry Leduc for my investigative piece. I'll call him on Monday and see if he's available."

"What about the third photo you took of Becca's business cards?"

"Right. The clinic." He searched online for Many Choices and clicked on the link to the website. "It's a medical clinic that offers a range of services. It's located in downtown Ottawa."

I read the text on the screen. "Contraceptive education... abortion care...testing for STIs—sexually transmitted infections..." My mind reeled with the implications. "Becca might have been pregnant and inquiring about getting an abortion. I wonder if Frank knows anything about this."

"I'm still wondering why he asked us if Becca had been alone in the hotel room." Michael shut his laptop. "So many questions."

I sat back in the sofa. "It's unbelievable how much information we can get from three little business cards, isn't it?"

His eyes gleamed. "And we haven't even started to dig yet."

7

After a noisy dinner in the Dorfin Hotel dining room, amplified by fidgety kids, crying babies, and toppled trays, the option of ordering our meals through room service was growing on me. I immediately said yes when Michael suggested we skip coffee and take the elevator up to the top floor lounge for a nightcap.

Based on the busy ambiance at dinner, I anticipated the bar would be a crowded and boisterous place too. After all, it was Saturday night.

It didn't disappoint. The dance floor was standing room only where patrons, young and not so young, made spasmodic attempts at moving to the pounding rhythm of the music. Colorful spears of light flashed in coordinated precision to the pulsating beats blasting from speakers.

We approached the bar. While three bartenders hastily prepared and served drinks, more people were waiting to place their orders. I could hardly hear the babble at the bar, let alone hear myself think. I wasn't going to last more than ten minutes here. Yet I didn't want to spoil Michael's evening by being a killjoy.

As we were waiting to order, someone grabbed my arm and shouted, "Hey there, honey. I thought I recognized you."

I instinctively yanked my arm back and spun around to see a familiar face. "Oh...hi...Roger!"

The odor of beer and his swaying stance told me he'd had more than his fair share of the brew. And he'd shared a lot of it with his shirt.

Michael put his arm around me and smiled amicably. His eyes, however, were troubled. "You having a good time, Roger?"

"Sure am! This place is filled to the brim with booze and babes." He held up a glass stein that was half full and spilled some on his shoes. "Oops!" He sniggered.

The pulsating music barely drowned out his garish laugh.

I hoped Michael wouldn't encourage any small talk with Roger, but it wasn't meant to be.

"Did you guys get another room?" Roger shouted at us over the din.

"Yes," Michael said. He looked over his shoulder and tried to get the attention of the bartender who was heading our way.

"I spoke to the detective about room 634," Roger said to me.

"That's good." Behind me, Michael was ordering our drinks. If Roger didn't move on soon, we certainly would.

"The detective thanked me." Roger beamed. "Especially for my witness statement about the woman. Did the cops find a dead body in that room?"

His loud voice caught stares from two young girls sitting at the bar next to him. They gaped at each other, took their drinks, and edged their way through the crowd to another spot.

"Not that I know of," I lied. In a way, it wasn't a lie. The detective didn't find the dead body in that room. Michael and I did.

"I was thinking," Roger said. "What if the dead body was that blonde I saw outside the room? The cops might think I killed her." He took a gulp of beer, gaping at me over the rim of his stein.

His gawk unnerved me.

Just then Michael held out a glass of sparkling white wine to me. "Here you go."

"Thanks." I took a sip.

"We're going to mingle," Michael said to Roger. "Have fun." He wrapped his arm around me and guided me through the crowd.

Not too soon, Roger claimed one of the vacant seats at the bar. Good. We wouldn't have to worry about him tailing us—at least for a while. "Thanks for rescuing me from Roger. He gives me the creeps."

"Yeah, guys like him have a tough time hitting it off with women."

"Gee, I wonder why."

"Now, Megan, be nice."

"The only man I want to be nice to is you." I smiled at him.

He chuckled. "That's good, because I'd fight off anyone who dared to come between us."

The room service attendant delivered brunch to our suite on Sunday. Dylan's black hotel vest and pants accentuated a tall, strapping physique topped with hair clipped close to his head at the back and sides. With white-gloved hands and a healthy dose of confidence, he effortlessly transferred serving plates from the food cart to the dining table.

Michael stood watching nearby. "You guys must be crazy busy these days," he said to him.

"With so many tourists in town, we can't even stop for breaks." Dylan placed cutlery and napkins neatly beside the plates. "It gets wild around here with requests for all kinds of services."

Perched on the sofa by the window, I listened in from time to time while I jotted notes for the local sites I needed to research for my ghostwriting project. The following days promised to be hectic.

Michael went on. "We were upstairs at the lounge last night and waited forever to get served. You ever worked at the bar?"

"Many times," Dylan said. "It pays well. I make my best tips there."

"Tell me. Can we order wine through room service? I mean, without a meal?"

I perked up. Michael was playing dumb—one of the methods he employed to draw information from unsuspecting sources. His easygoing style often worked to his advantage.

"Yes, you can order wine without a meal," Dylan said. "They accept orders for food and beverages until nine at night."

Michael lowered his voice. "There's another reason I mentioned the wine. I noticed a service trolley parked near room 634 on Friday between five-thirty and six o'clock."

Dylan paused as he reached for a hot plate, his gloved hands resting on the silver handles. "Oh. That was probably me. I had the early Friday evening run." He transferred the plate to the table.

Michael kept his voice low. "I walked by and the door to that room was open. I couldn't help noticing the woman in there. Blonde. Hot."

Dylan gave him a brief smile but said nothing. He kept setting the table.

In case Dylan happened to look my way, I flipped through the pages of my notebook and pretended I wasn't listening.

Michael persisted. "So did you see her?"

"No, the room was empty when I delivered the wine." Dylan stopped. He'd evidently caught his slip-up about mentioning the wine but recovered in the next moment. "She must have checked in right after."

"You sure missed something." Michael chuckled.

Dylan dropped a metal plate cover. The clatter resounded

in the spacious room. He quickly bent over to pick it up. "Sorry about that."

"No problem," Michael said. "What I was getting at about the woman..." He spoke softly. "Do you think you could, you know, introduce me to her?"

"I can't."

"Why not?"

"Because she left."

"She checked out?"

"Not exactly."

I peeked at the men.

Michael hadn't budged. Dylan stood facing him with a deadpan expression.

Michael dug out a fifty-dollar bill and held it out to Dylan. "What else can you tell me about the occupant of room 634?"

Dylan took the bill and slipped it in his pocket. "The regular client is a high roller. He can afford the room. He works for the fat cats in Ottawa. He's been on the hotel roster for years. Female guests visit his room from time to time."

"Hookers?"

"I don't ask and don't want to know."

His flippant attitude didn't deter Michael. "Who ordered the wine?"

"I don't know. It could have been the regular occupant or the guest. Guests are granted a limited expense account during their stay there."

"I'd like to know who ordered the wine." Michael slipped him another bill.

Dylan made it disappear. "I'll see what I can find out."

"What happened to the woman in room 634 on Friday?"

Dylan hesitated. "I don't know. It was busy. There were lots of people going back and forth in the hallway and—"

"Stop playing games. The cops spoke to you about the dead woman, right?"

"Yes." Dylan placed the last of the dishes on the table.

"And?"

"The word is she overdosed. You didn't hear this from me."

"Any idea where she could have gotten the drugs?"

Dylan glared at him. "How am I supposed to know? I only deliver food and drinks, not drugs."

Michael crossed his arms and waited.

"You can try the ByWard Market," Dylan said. "The place is supposed to be crawling with dealers."

"How about closer to home? Like right here in the hotel."

Dylan bristled. "Everybody knows someone who deals."

"Do you?"

"I might. You interested?"

Michael ignored his question. "Anything else you can tell me about the woman? Was she a regular guest here?"

Dylan shook his head. "Like I said, I didn't see her. I don't keep tabs on the comings and goings of guests either. Enjoy your meal." He hurried out the door.

I picked at the plump strawberries on my plate. My appetite had dwindled despite the spread of scrumptious dishes on the table and the heavenly aroma emanating from them. Dylan's casual replies to Michael's questions had unnerved me.

Michael was his usual self, enjoying his share of buttered pancakes, strips of bacon, and hash browns. Stressful events only increased his desire to refuel.

"What do you make of Dylan?" I asked him. "Do you think he's telling the truth?"

"I hit a nerve when I talked to him about Becca. It rattled him. Hard to tell if it was due to what happened in room 634 or if he's involved in some way."

"Involved? How?"

"Maybe he saw someone or something suspicious but decided to keep it under wraps."

I took a sip of coffee. "What's that saying about bad news traveling fast? It sure can't beat the speed of gossip in this hotel. For the right price, of course." I gave him a wry smile.

"Money talks," Michael said between forkfuls of hash browns. "As long as it serves the purpose, I don't mind dishing it out."

I could attest to that firsthand. Coming from a wealthy family, Michael had turned his back on a lifestyle of leisure in exchange for one that satisfied his quest for justice—not to mention his penchant for taking risks. The money he paid out to informants represented a proverbial drop in the bucket of prosperity he would one day inherit.

"At least Dylan confirmed what Eric had already told us," I said. "The regular occupant of room 634 has connections to the fat cats in Ottawa."

"In my book, that translates to either politics or business, or both," Michael said.

"We also learned that he's a high roller who invites female friends over." I echoed an earlier premise. "I refuse to think like Detective Grist that Becca Landry was working in the oldest profession on earth."

"The real mystery is how she ended up in that room. What we have to find out is the name of the regular occupant."

"Why didn't you ask Dylan?"

"He wouldn't have told me. The guy is a tattletale, but he needs his day job."

"What about asking your tech friend?"

"He asked me to give him a couple of days to dig up the other stuff. If I don't hear from him by then, I'll give him a call." He leaned back, placed a hand on his flat stomach. "This meal was just what I needed. Let's go outdoors later. See the sights. Take some photos."

I sat up. "You mean, for my ghostwriting project?"

Michael tilted his head so-so. "Well, not exactly..."

"Oh. For your investigative article then."

"Well..."

Something told me he had more in mind than sightseeing. "It's okay, Michael. You can tell me what you're really up to."

He gave me a sheepish grin. "What do you mean?"

"You're researching the illegal drug market. I can only imagine what you have in mind."

He laughed. "You read me so well. I wanted to check out the ByWard Market and—" His phone rang and he answered. He listened intently during the brief conversation. "Okay," he said before ending the call.

"Who's the mystery caller?"

"Frank Landry. He asked us to drive over to his home. He received the preliminary autopsy report on Becca and needs our help. The guy was crying so hard, he could barely speak."

8

My heart pounded as Michael pulled into Frank's driveway. I was surprised that Frank had included me in his plea for help, but maybe he had his own reasons for doing so. I'd find out soon enough.

The dark circles under his bloodshot eyes meant he hadn't had much sleep lately. From what Michael had gathered during their earlier phone conversation, his wife's autopsy results would no doubt cause the widower more sleepless nights.

Frank ushered us into the living room. "My mother is in the backyard with the kids. I didn't want her to overhear us talking. It would kill her if she knew what I found out about Becca."

Uh-oh. Not what I wanted to hear. I braced myself for dismal news.

Frank began. "The coroner's office came by this morning to give me the preliminary results of Becca's autopsy. They said the probable cause of death was some kind of drug overdose."

I gasped. "Oh, no."

"Did they say what drug?" Michael asked him.

Frank shook his head. "They'll know more after they analyze the final results."

A tense moment of silence ensued.

"Did they tell you anything else?"

Frank avoided his gaze and stared at the floor. "Becca was pregnant."

His revelation came as a complete surprise.

The squealing sounds of children playing outdoors filtered through an open window, as if to serve as a reminder of what might have been.

I spoke softly. "Did you know Becca was pregnant?"

"Hell, no." Frank ran a hand through his hair.

"Were you planning on having more children?"

"We hadn't discussed it. I would have welcomed another child." Tears welled in his eyes and he blinked them away. "What gets me is that they found drugs in her system. If Becca knew she was pregnant, she would never have taken drugs. Something's not right."

"How far along was she in the pregnancy?"

"Three months." His shoulders sagged in despair. "I trusted her. I would have given my life for her. Yet she didn't trust me enough to tell me she was pregnant."

Anger washed over his face and settled in the corners of his mouth. Becca's autopsy results bothered him, but I sensed that something else was nagging at him.

Michael picked up on it too. "Have you told us everything, Frank?"

"Not quite." He cringed, as if his next words would cause pain. "Ever since I returned from my tour of duty, Becca was distant. We basically lived like strangers in the same house." He gaped at us. "You want to know the truth? I don't even know if the baby she was carrying was mine."

His comment stunned me. "Why would you say that?"

Frank hesitated. "I thought she was sleeping around."

Michael cut short an awkward moment. "Did she give you reason to think so?"

"Let me explain." Frank glanced over his shoulder to make

sure the rest of his household was still outdoors. "Becca came from a broken home. She was raised by an alcoholic mother. She earned money the only way she could when she was old enough. She was working for an escort service when I first met her."

His revelation stunned me. Detective Grist had implied that Becca was a "working girl" and I had called him out on it.

Most of all, Frank's disclosure had stirred my curiosity. Had Becca gone back to her old ways? And if so, why?

Michael raised a hand. "Frank, you don't have to—"

"I'm not finished." Frank shifted in his chair. "When we first met, I took Becca out to dinner a few times. I saw the goodness in her heart and persuaded her to give up her lifestyle. After we got married and had Cory and Olivia, my mother took up our offer and moved in with us. She even helped pay the bills. Becca loved being home with the kids, but she wanted to work to contribute her share. She applied for job after job but fell short. All she had was a high school diploma, and she'd never worked in an office before. About a year ago, she got a lucky break. A company that did contract work for non-government organizations hired her. I couldn't have been prouder."

"Was she working at the same job when...?" I let my words trail off.

"Yes, till the end." He sniffed.

"Were you working during that time?"

"Like I told you, I returned home with a leg injury seven months ago. Things got worse when I couldn't land a job—not even a part-time one. After a while, Becca began to complain about her job. She worked long hours. Whenever I tried to get close to her, she wouldn't let me touch her. I thought, maybe, just maybe, she'd gone back to her old ways."

Such unfounded suspicions! I couldn't hide my frustration. "That's a stretch. Why would you suspect that Becca was cheating on you? Maybe she was exhausted from working long hours."

"I was jobless and had a bum leg," Frank said. "I wasn't the man she'd married."

"She married you for better or for worse," Michael said.

"Well, she got the worse part of me," Frank shot back. "We were struggling to make ends meet. It's not as if she was raking it in either. She only made twenty-five thousand dollars a year."

Michael nodded. "I get you. Lack of money can put strain on a marriage."

"Damn right," Frank said. "We'd have the worst arguments about money. You don't know how much I regret those stupid fights now." He stopped, remembering. "When Becca didn't answer my calls at the hotel Friday night, I imagined all sorts of things. Like maybe she'd dumped me for someone else."

"If that were true," I said, "she wouldn't have asked you to pack a bag and meet her at the hotel."

"I thought hard about that, believe me," Frank said. "Becca told me that same afternoon that she had something important to discuss with me. I didn't know if it was good or bad. Like I said, my imagination went wild when I couldn't reach her. I thought we were finished...that she'd left town."

I tried to understand it from Becca's viewpoint. "Maybe she wanted to meet with you to tell you about her pregnancy."

"I doubt it. The detective told me she had two thousand dollars in cash on her. He asked me if she was planning a trip. What do you think went through my mind?"

I'd almost forgotten about the money in Becca's purse.

"On top of that, how the hell did she manage to pay for a weekend at the hotel? We couldn't afford to spend that kind of money." Creases rippled his forehead.

Michael leaned forward. "I don't mean to pry in your personal finances, Frank, but did you and Becca share a bank account?"

"Yes. We had a joint account between us since the day we got married. Every transaction went through it, including Becca's pay, my medical insurance benefits, and most of the bills. We didn't keep that kind of information from each other —as far as I know."

"How can we help you, Frank?"

What? Why would he want to help this man? All I saw was a husband who believed his wife had cheated on him but had no evidence to prove it. Had I missed something here?

I held back from voicing my thoughts—if only because I believed in Michael's instincts as an investigative journalist.

"You can help me by keeping the cops out of my life," Frank said.

"They're investigating your wife's death," Michael said. "Why would you want to stop them?"

"Because I don't trust cops."

"Why not?"

Frank rubbed a hand along his thigh. "Grist knows Becca's history as an escort."

Michael stared at him in surprise. "What?"

I needed to be sure. "Detective Grist knew Becca?"

"Yes," Frank said. "From way back. He knew she'd had a run-in with a client years ago. It got ugly when the client refused to pay her after she escorted him to a dinner event. Now that Grist is on board..." He rubbed his brow. "The way things are going, it's only a matter of time before he starts looking in my direction."

Michael asked, "Don't you think you're jumping the gun? Grist hasn't given you any indication it was a homicide, has he?"

"Not yet," Frank said. "He thinks Becca killed herself. That'll change once the final autopsy reports come in. Then he'll finger me for murder."

"It sounds like your mind is made up."

"Becca wasn't suicidal. As much as I thought she was going to leave me, she wouldn't have killed herself."

Michael focused on Frank and said nothing. I'd come to know this other maneuver as his preferred strategy to draw out more information.

"Look, Becca didn't have any fancy certificates or university degrees to her name," Frank said, "but she was smart enough to know when she was being duped. Somebody killed her before she could tell me what was going on."

Michael sat back. "Why did you ask us to come here?"

Frank gave him a measured look. "I checked your credentials. You've handled your share of tough crime investigations. I'd like you to find out more about my wife's coworkers and friends. Somebody must know something."

"So think back. Did Becca ever say anything that might indicate someone had threatened her at work or anywhere else?"

"Nothing." He paused. "I might have a lead though." He looked at me. "The detective asked me if I knew about a clinic Becca might have visited. A women's clinic. It's called Many Choices. I can't walk into a place like that without raising suspicions."

Many Choices. It was the name on a business card in Becca's purse. "So you want me to go there and pretend I'm asking for information?"

"Exactly. I have a bit of money for my mortgage payments and car insurance. I'll gladly pay you both whatever—"

"Keep your money," Michael said. "If Megan and I agree to help you, you have to agree to respect certain conditions. You have to be upfront with us. If you lie or mislead us, the deal is off. If you commit a crime, we won't go to jail for you."

Frank held out his hand. "You've got a deal."

Michael took me on a stroll through the Dorfin Hotel later that afternoon to assess the scope of the surveillance system on the premises. We determined that the closed-circuit coverage included the lobby and elevators. We didn't detect cameras in the hallways on any of the floors that housed guests.

As we made our way along the underground parking area,

Michael scanned the perimeter. "There's a surveillance system down here too. If we can get a copy of the hotel video, we'll have no problem proving Frank's alibi. There'll be a timestamp showing the time he arrived and the time he left."

"If he's telling the truth," I said.

"Why the cynicism?"

"Isn't it obvious? He's so ready to believe that Becca cheated on him, he won't even give her the benefit of the doubt."

"What if she *was* cheating on him?"

"Then he'd have the motive and opportunity to kill her, wouldn't he? And maybe the means."

Michael raised a forefinger. "You're jumping to conclusions, Megan. It's important in my line of work not to assign guilt to a potential suspect until I have tangible evidence to back it up."

"I understand, but think about this. Did you ever wonder why Frank didn't call the police when he couldn't reach Becca that Friday evening?"

"She wasn't technically missing. If Frank thought she'd left town—and him—he wouldn't have called the police."

He had a point. "Okay. I'll try to keep an open mind."

As soon as we returned to our suite, Michael's phone rang. He answered. "No, not too busy. What can I do for you?" He mouthed the name Grist.

I mouthed no.

Michael shrugged in response.

I let it go. If anything, Michael was polite. He wouldn't snub the detective simply because I thought the man was annoying. And a touch arrogant.

After a brief conversation that involved several grunts of affirmation, Michael said to him, "Okay, I'll see what I can do." He ended the call. "Guess what? Grist asked me to do some investigative research for him. He'll even foot the bill."

"Aha! I knew it! Didn't I tell you he'd drag you into doing his legwork for him?" I turned and stormed into the living room.

Michael followed me and placed his phone on the coffee table. "He hasn't dragged me into anything yet."

I folded my arms. "What does he want?"

"He wants me to be his eyes and ears at the hotel. Report any details I happen to come across regarding 'the incident' in room 634." He made air quotes around the words.

"Why does he think of you as his lapdog? Doesn't he have resources to do his dirty work for him?"

"Not on site. Definitely not on a twenty-four seven basis."

"What about our deal with Frank? He doesn't trust the police, remember?"

Michael put his hands on my shoulders. "Don't worry. I'll only tell Grist what he needs to know. In the meantime, what do you say we head out?"

"What do you have in mind?"

"Let's go for a walk in the ByWard Market. Grab dinner at one of the better restaurants there. Visit the sites."

"Why do I sense an ulterior reason?"

"Okay, you got me." He smiled. "I'd like to check out the drug scene on the streets tonight. See how bad it really is."

"Is that wise?"

"No problem. There'll be a lot of people around. I promise it won't be dangerous."

Famous last words.

9

—————

After a steak dinner at The Keg on York Street, Michael and I strolled through the ByWard Market. The outdoor four-block square was home to dozens of street vendors selling everything from potted flowers to maple syrup to jewelry, all under canvas awnings. Cafés, specialty food shops, boutiques, galleries, and entertainment venues made me wish we'd planned a longer visit.

We'd parked the car blocks away before dinner, with the intention to tackle the market on foot afterward. Throngs of people had the same idea and now extended their trek from the crowded sidewalks to the busy streets. The intermittent honking of horns sounded from impatient drivers who inched their vehicles through the measured flow of pedestrians.

The sun was setting as we neared the edge of the ByWard Market. We hadn't completed our tour of the area, but many shops had closed down or were in the process of doing so. With one notable exception.

The window of a marijuana dispensary displayed cannabis-laced brownies, cookies, teas, and candy shaped like teddy bears. The pungent odor of cannabis hit me as we sauntered by the open door.

"Ugh!" I put a hand over my nose. "It might be considered cool to smoke pot, but it sure stinks!"

"It's not even legal to sell it here," Michael said. "The federal government hasn't legalized the sale of recreational marijuana yet."

"If it's against the law, how are they getting away with it?"

"Simple. The cops don't enforce the law."

"Why not?"

"They usually act on complaints from the public. Sometimes they investigate places, raid them, and shut them down. Sometimes they don't."

"Doctors prescribe medical marijuana to their patients. Where do they get their supplies?"

"From producers licensed by Health Canada. Even if pot shops like this one sell it, they might not be meeting the legal criteria."

We passed two teens smoking in front of another dispensary. They couldn't have been older than fifteen.

I whispered to Michael, "I don't see how smoking pot and frying your brain cells at a young age can be healthy."

"Don't get me started."

Along the sidewalk, streetlights glowed against a darkened sky. The crowds had disappeared. Only a trickle of window shoppers remained, occasionally stopping to peek inside the stores.

A chilly gust of wind sent shivers down my neck. "It's getting late. Let's go back to the car."

Michael didn't answer but kept staring across the street.

"What is it?"

"I just saw a drug dealer make a sale. The pot shops aren't the only game in town." He slipped his hand in mine. "Okay. Let's go back to the hotel."

As we passed a shadowy alley between buildings, I noticed two people sitting there, staring into oblivion, their eyes vacant.

Although Michael and I were in no obvious danger, what I'd witnessed was disturbing and made me feel queasy. I wished we'd left the area sooner.

We hadn't covered more than half a block when a shrill scream pierced the air.

"Help! Somebody, help!" a woman shouted from across the street. She was kneeling over a man sprawled on the sidewalk.

Michael let go of my hand and ran over.

I rushed after him, my pulse racing.

Up close, the young woman didn't look older than sixteen. The young man was about the same age.

"My boyfriend passed out!" She looked up at us, tears streaming down her face. "I don't know what's wrong with him. Please help him!"

Michael checked the boy's breathing and pulse. He pulled out his phone and handed it to me. "Call 911. His breathing is shallow. " He immediately performed CPR on the teen.

My hand was shaking as I contacted the police.

The dispatcher came on the line.

I explained the situation and gave her our location. She asked for my name and Michael's. When she asked for the victim's name, I activated the speakerphone to put the teenage girl on. I kept a firm grip on the phone so the girl wouldn't have to. She was in bad enough shape already.

Caitlin gave out her personal information but struggled as she tried to recall her boyfriend Jacob's address and phone number. "I–I don't remember. Wait!" She frantically fished her phone from her handbag, only to fumble and drop it. It cracked along one edge but was otherwise intact. Still sobbing, she retrieved his contact information and passed it on to the dispatcher.

"Does Jacob have a health condition that you know of?" the

dispatcher asked her. "Is he taking any medications that you're aware of?"

"No." Caitlin wiped her eyes with the back of her hand, leaving smudges of mascara across her cheeks.

"Has he been doing drugs?"

She hesitated. "Yes."

"Which drugs?"

"I don't know. It was a small blue pill."

"What was it?"

"I don't know!"

"Does he have any more pills on him?"

Caitlin stuck a hand in Jacob's jacket and pulled out a tiny packet of pills. "Yes."

The thought that the pills might have been opioids laced with fentanyl crossed my mind. I made a mental note to ask Michael about it later.

A handful of people had gathered around us, whispering, gawking.

All the while, Michael had kept up the chest compressions.

This alarming situation called for nothing less than intense focus and nerves of steel. I had focus, but nerves of steel? Not my forte. A fleeting thought about how brave Michael was at this exact moment crossed my mind but vanished as sirens approached.

A male paramedic and his female colleague jumped from the ambulance and tended to Jacob within seconds. They functioned with precision as they assessed his condition. Then the female paramedic pulled out a syringe and injected him.

"She gave him a shot of naloxone," Michael whispered to me. "It's a medication that temporarily reverses the effects of opioid overdose. It works within seconds."

But nothing happened.

"Oh, my God!" Caitlin put a hand to her mouth. "What's wrong? Is he dying? Do something!"

The male paramedic asked Caitlin, "Do you have the pills?"

"Yes." She handed them over.

He studied them. "Let's give him another shot," he said to his colleague.

A second dose of the antidote instantly brought Jacob back to consciousness. He sat up, stunned by all the people around him. "What the hell?"

Caitlin squeezed his hand. "Oh, my God, Jacob. You almost died. Don't you remember anything?"

Jacob shook his head. "I remember you walking beside me and then... nothing."

I was trembling. The incident had jolted me. I'd witnessed a teen on the brink of death, only to be brought back to life by the paramedics within moments. What if Michael and I hadn't been close by to hear Caitlin's cry for help? The girl had clearly been too distraught to even think of dialling 911.

Claps and cheers erupted from a crowd that had doubled in size since I'd last looked around. People snapped shots of us with their phones and held a thumps-up in our direction.

Michael approached the paramedics. "Thank you for your help. The fentanyl epidemic must keep you guys pretty busy."

The female paramedic said, "We sometimes work twenty hours a day and can barely respond to the number of emergency calls we get."

"The doctors and nurses have the same problem," the other paramedic said. "Staff shortage."

Their task completed, they lifted Jacob onto a stretcher and into the ambulance.

Caitlin brushed away fresh tears as she approached Michael and me. She thanked us repeatedly before she climbed into the ambulance and rode off with Jacob to the hospital.

With the excitement over, people slowly moved away.

I hugged Michael. "I'm so proud of you. You're such a hero."

"Anyone could have done what I did," he said.

"I'm not so sure about that."

He smiled. "Let's go back to the hotel before my head starts to swell from all the attention."

"Let's see." I touched the back of his head. "Nope. Nothing's changed yet." I giggled.

"You're a riot, Megan, you know that?" He drew me close and kissed me.

We walked in silence for a while, breathing in the cool night air, each lost in our own thoughts.

"Michael, do you think Jacob will be okay?"

"The doctors will run some tests on him," he said. "Whether or not the kid decides to play Russian roulette with street drugs again is his decision."

"I meant to ask you earlier. Do you think the pills Jacob took were opioids laced with fentanyl?"

"Maybe. If he got them from drug-traffickers on the street, it's even possible they were counterfeit pills laced with fentanyl. All he needed was a dose of fentanyl the size of a grain of sand to kill him."

"Good thing naloxone works so fast on opioid users. Jacob could have died without this kind of intervention."

"No kidding."

Michael's phone rang. He retrieved it from his pocket. "It's my tech friend. He's probably got something for me." His eyes sparkled the way they always did when exciting developments surfaced during one of his investigations.

The call triggered my curiosity too.

~

Michael slid next to me on the sofa in our hotel suite, then set up his laptop on the coffee table. "Can't wait to see what he sent me."

He never called his tech friend by name—not even to me— though he'd once hinted that their friendship hailed from their university days together. Michael was the sort of person who kept in touch with old friends over the years. He believed the value of loyal connections reaped rewards on both sides.

Michael had procured his tech friend's services for other investigative cases that involved breaking into computer systems. All in the name of justice, of course. I suspected that his friend worked for a government security group or a high-tech company, but Michael remained tight-lipped about it. As an investigative journalist, he was strict about protecting his sources, no matter who they were. I left it at that.

Michael peered at the screen. "Take a look at this."

I leaned forward. Words ran down one column and numbers ran down the others. "What kind of report is that?"

"The hotel keycard activity record covering the specific time of entry in room 634." He scrolled down the list. "There's an entry for housekeeping at four-thirty Friday afternoon. Another one at five-thirty for room service."

"According to what Dylan told us, that last one must have been the wine delivery. What time did Becca arrive?"

"The next customer activation is at quarter to six. It had to be her."

"We already know Frank stepped into the hotel lobby at six Friday evening and left at seven."

Michael met my gaze. "Becca could have been dead before Frank arrived."

"If you're right, she wouldn't have had much time to be with another man—whether she was having an affair or working as an escort."

"We need more proof." He pulled out his phone. "I'll text my friend and ask him to get into the hotel's surveillance video system. I'll narrow the time frame to make it easier for him."

"What if he can't access the system?"

A smile spread across his face. "He's never let me down so far. If we're lucky, the video from the hotel lobby and parking garage will support Frank's alibi. It'll also cancel his unfounded fears about being the prime suspect in his wife's death."

"Oh... Don't forget to ask your friend to track down the name of the regular occupant in room 634."

"Right. Thanks for reminding me. That detail could turn out to be an important lead."

"All the better for our investigation."

Then why was I so uneasy about what we'd discover?

10

Our encounter with Jacob in the ByWard Market increased my curiosity about how special interest groups were helping to curtail the city's drug epidemic. To that end, my Monday morning was free, so I asked Michael if I could accompany him to his two meetings. He agreed.

Randall Thorne reminded me of a boardroom CEO I'd once met. A man in his late fifties, he wore a stylish suit that obscured a fleshy waist. Though he displayed a rigid demeanor, the skepticism in his eyes defied you to impress him.

I was glad I'd changed into a dress and heels and persuaded Michael to wear a jacket and tie. Nothing beat a professional appearance when it came to dealing with corporate types—even for a fifteen-minute meeting.

The head of Addiction Recovery Foundation invited us to sit in comfy chairs in his office for our nine o'clock get-together. His desk was free of clutter, except for a pen and a notepad, giving the impression that he was rarely in this downtown office in the glass-panel building on Metcalfe Street.

True to form, Randall Thorne made short work of small talk. "What can I do for you?"

Michael began. "As I mentioned on the phone, Megan and I are gathering information about the current drug crisis. Can you tell us what role your foundation plays in curtailing drug abuse, Mr. Thorne?"

"Call me Randall." His voice, a deep baritone, made it sound as if it were a command rather than a suggestion. "One of the tasks of our advisory group is to educate the public about substance abuse. As you probably know, Ottawa is experiencing an epidemic of opioid-related deaths. Numerous deaths by opioid overdose have involved fentanyl. In fact, considering the number of overdose deaths from coast to coast, the federal government has stated the crisis is a national concern."

I joined the conversation. "How is your organization educating the public about fentanyl?"

"We have numerous avenues available," Randall said. "We use training resources to create drug prevention programs for businesses, educational groups, and the like. For example, specific programs warn against purchasing illegal fentanyl from street vendors. Drug dealers often sell their own concoction of the drug and don't care who dies from it."

"Like fentanyl-laced heroin," Michael said. "It's the solution for drug users searching for a stronger high."

Randall nodded. "Precisely. The addition of fentanyl increases the potency or compensates for the low-quality heroin they use."

"They sell it under names like green apples, greenies, and eighties. Users can buy one drug but find out later that it's something else."

"Exactly. I see you've done your homework." He smiled. "The Ottawa Police recently arrested dozens of people in a ring suspected of distributing fentanyl-laced pills. They seized a load of pills and confiscated assault rifles and handguns in the process."

I rejoined the discussion. "What about measures to stop the entry of these drugs into the country?"

"Excellent question," Randall said. "The government is taking steps to ban the illegal entry of these drugs since they account for the bulk of transactions on the street. Our goal is to educate the public before they get their hands on them."

"If opioid users happen to overdose, there's naloxone," Michael said.

"Undeniably," Randall said. "The Peer Overdose Prevention Program put naloxone into the hands of qualified people. Law enforcement officers and firefighters are trained to use naloxone kits to reverse the effects of opioid overdose. Through our national programs, we're spreading the word that even users should carry this antidote on them in case of overdose. Time is of the essence in such situations."

Michael told him about our experience last night in the ByWard Market and Jacob's brush with death. I shuddered involuntarily as I relived that horrible moment.

"Young people take needless risks." Randall pursed his lips. "The medical community warns people under twenty-five years of age about the potential side effects of smoking pot. The danger is magnified when they go looking for something stronger."

"Like fentanyl," Michael said.

Randall fingered the pen on his desk. "We occasionally hear about teens holding house parties in affluent suburbs. They can't do drugs in public areas without being seen, so it's a way to hide their usage—especially if their parents aren't around."

"It must be hard on parents," I said. "They trust their kids to do the right thing and not risk their lives."

A frown deepened the wrinkles in Randall's forehead. "I've met many worried parents at drug prevention meetings. They find hope through our programs. We show them how to see the signs before they lose their kids to drugs."

"Sounds like a timely platform," Michael said. "Would you mind sharing the names of the resources you use? I'd like to interview them for my article."

"Of course. Anything that will help share vital information." Randall gave him a brief smile. "We deal mainly with Jerry Leduc of Looking Ahead. Jerry's group is highly involved in offering learning programs to drug addicts who want to turn their lives around and are seeking employment. I can also recommend..."

I stopped listening. Looking Ahead, where Becca had worked, kept popping up in our conversations. Was it just a coincidence?

Michael continued his line of questioning. "Randall, how does your organization determine the success rate of the learning programs?"

"By the number of successful graduates. The Public Health Agency and other sponsors have increased their financial support over the years based on the rising number of diplomas issued to graduates."

Michael smiled. "That's good to hear."

I checked the time. We needed to raise the topic of Becca Landry. I took the leap. "We'd like to discuss another topic that might be drug related. When Michael and I walked into our hotel room in town this weekend, we discovered the body of a young woman in our room."

Color drained from Randall's face. "Would that happen to be the Dorfin Hotel?"

I was stunned. "Yes. How did you know?"

He shifted in his chair. "A police detective left here minutes before you arrived. He told me he's investigating the death of a woman at that hotel."

"Was it Detective Grist?"

"Yes, that's the name. I had to rush back to town from my weekend hunting trip to answer his questions." His lips tightened, indicating that the detective's intrusion had caused him a major inconvenience.

I was baffled. If Detective Grist believed Becca had killed herself, why was he interviewing witnesses?

Invasion of privacy or not, I had to ask. "Did you know the deceased woman?"

"No," Randall said. "Apparently, there was a connection to my foundation, but her name isn't familiar to me."

I winged it. "She had your business card in her purse and we thought..." I counted on him to finish the sentence.

"Yes. The detective did mention something of the sort." He eyed me with a modicum of caution. "The fact is I happen to be a well-known fixture within various levels of bureaucracy. My foundation does contract work for government departments and treatment centers across the country. I travel on a regular basis, and thousands of my business cards are handed out from coast to coast. Perhaps the young woman got hold of one of them somehow."

"And applied for a job with your foundation."

"Like I said, her name is unfamiliar to me." Randall tapped his fingers on the armchair rests.

Why was he so impatient? It wasn't as if we'd exceeded our time limit.

Maybe the detective's visit had unnerved him, caused him to worry about his reputation. So much for maintaining a cool façade under pressure. On the other hand, it wasn't every day that the business card of a reputable administrator was found in a dead woman's purse.

"You mentioned a drug overdose," Randall said to me. "I don't recall the police saying anything about that."

"No, I said her death might be drug related."

"Oh."

"It's just a theory at this point," Michael said. "The police investigation has to take its course."

"Without question," Randall agreed. "However, as you can see, the subject of drug abuse is always on my mind." He pushed himself out of his chair. "I'm sorry, but I have to attend another meeting. I trust I've contributed to your research article on fentanyl, Michael. If you have any more questions, don't hesitate to send me an email." He handed him his business card.

Once outside the building, I said to Michael, "Did you notice how agitated Randall became when we questioned him about Becca?"

"These quasi bureaucrats have to be careful. Everything they do is in the public eye. If word gets out to the media and they link Randall to Becca's death because of a simple business card, it could trigger a scandal."

And in this city—like any nation's capital—even a scandal involving a quasi bureaucrat could have widespread political repercussions.

11

Lucky for us, Jerry Leduc's office building was only two blocks away from Randall's. We left the car in the parking lot and covered the distance on foot.

Michael hadn't called to make an appointment, preferring to use the element of surprise instead. He had a hunch we wouldn't be turned away.

As we headed to our destination, I related my suspicions about Detective Grist. "If he interviewed Randall, it could mean he's investigating Becca's death as a murder now."

"Then let's hope he doesn't get to Jerry Leduc's office before us. Otherwise we'll have to play catch-up if we want to clear Frank's name."

Wearing high heels while trying to keep up with Michael was a challenge. His eagerness to get to Jerry Leduc's office explained why he was practically jogging.

I placed a hand on his arm. "Can you slow down a little? It's tough to run in high heels."

"Oh. Sorry, Megan." He reduced his pace. "Anyway, about Becca... Frank is certain she was murdered. I trust the guy's instincts."

We entered a low-rise 1960s building on Metcalfe Street and rode the elevator up to the fourth floor. If Detective Grist hadn't yet arrived at Jerry Leduc's office, the timing of our meeting with the owner of Looking Ahead would give us an advantage. If the detective was already there, we'd have a difficult time explaining our arrival.

As soon as we entered the reception area, my stomach did a flip-flop.

Detective Grist was standing by an employee's computer at the front desk, pen and notebook in hand.

It was too late. We couldn't walk back out. How on earth were we supposed to explain the purpose of our visit?

Surprise flashed across the detective's face when he noticed us. He abandoned his post and walked up to us. "Well, we meet again. What brings you here?"

"Research for my article." Michael lowered his voice. "I'm following a lead regarding 'the incident' in room 634. I saw the name of this organization on a business card."

Awareness gleamed in the detective's eyes. "Ah...yes. Good move." His phone rang. "Excuse me." He took the call, then turned and hurried down a corridor that most likely led to the staff offices.

A young woman in heels a lot higher than mine entered the reception area and approached us. "How can I help you?"

Michael handed her Randall's business card. "My associate and I just came out of a meeting with Randall Thorne. He recommended that we speak with Jerry Leduc."

She took a quick look at the card and returned it to Michael. "Please have a seat. It won't be long."

I'd barely had time to observe the thick carpeting and the dark oak panels lining the walls when the young woman in heels returned.

"Mr. Leduc will see you now. Please come with me."

As Michael and I followed her along the corridor, I peeked into the offices. I counted four cubicles set off by glass partitions. There was no employee in any of the offices and no trace of Detective Grist either.

In the next cubicle, a woman sat dabbing her eyes with a tissue. I didn't give it a second thought until I passed another cubicle where two women stood speaking in hushed tones, their faces blotchy.

We passed a closed office on the right that had glass walls from top to bottom. No one was in there.

The next office was on the left of the corridor and had the same glass walls. The receptionist stopped at the entrance and tapped lightly on the open door.

A man in a jacket and tie sat behind a desk. He was on the phone, and judging from the scowl on his face and his hand motions, the discussion was intense. He noticed us, hastily completed the call, then fumbled with the cell phone and dropped it on his desk. He stood up and smiled, then adjusted his tie over a rounded stomach. As he sauntered toward us, the weight of his torso swayed from side to side atop short legs.

After handshakes and introductions, Jerry admitted he was more comfortable on a first-name basis. "Please, have a seat, Michael," he said as if to make his point, and yet he omitted my name. "I understand that Randall Thorne sent you to see me."

"He didn't send us here," Michael said, "though he did mention your organization and how you've worked together on projects."

A smile skimmed across Jerry's lips. "You don't say? Well, that was nice of him." He examined the top of his desk, scooped up a flash drive, and slipped it in his pocket. "So how can I help you?"

"I'm writing a four-part exposé on drug abuse for *The Gazette* in Montreal," Michael said.

"I gather this isn't a trivial piece," Jerry said. "It sounds like serious stuff."

"It is."

While Michael explained his research project, I surveyed

the spacious office. Sports paraphernalia like bike goggles, red baseball caps sporting the white Canada 150 crest on the front, and tennis balls filled a six-tiered rack in the far right corner. To the left of it, photos of sports celebrities, water bottles, and different colored T-shirts formed piles on a rectangular table. I assumed Jerry handed out these items to prospective clients.

"I'm interested in finding out how organizations are fighting against drug abuse," Michael was saying. "Tell me the role that Looking Ahead plays in the growing crisis."

"To begin with, it took me decades to build up this firm." Jerry raised his fleshy chin with pride. "We employ a staff of five. Educational instructors, writers, and other professionals work on contract off-site. We depend on government funds and public contributions to subsidize our operations. We organize fundraisers for charities, do event planning, and develop many e-learning courses."

"What are some of the subjects in your courses?"

He motioned to a stack of guidebooks on his desk. "We offer a range of subjects, from drug abuse in teenagers to medication overdose in seniors." He took the top two guidebooks and placed them on the desk so we could see them better.

I reached for one of the guidebooks and flipped through it. Colored photos and illustrations filled the bulk of the pages. "You obviously put a lot of work into the production of these books."

Jerry nodded. "It takes about six months to produce each course. We synchronize production with consultants, designers, editors... Whatever it takes."

Michael had more questions. "What type of work does your firm do for non-governmental groups—like the one Randall Thorne runs?"

"We do a lot of work with private addiction centers. We create programs that help secure jobs for drug addicts after they've cleaned up. Basically, we show our applicants how to prepare employee résumés and job applications."

"My article highlights fentanyl abuse. Do you have any courses on that?"

"We developed one to meet requests for information about the growing crisis." Jerry ran his stubby fingers along the spines of the guidebooks. He tugged on a thin booklet, causing three books above it to slide to the floor. "Oh, damn!"

I leaned over and picked them up. In the process, I noticed a letter-sized box under Jerry's desk. A sheet of paper taped to the cover of the box had an official-looking gold seal on it, like the sort applied to a diploma or certificate. I sat up and placed the toppled guidebooks on Jerry's desk.

"Thank you. I'm all thumbs today." Jerry let out a nervous laugh, then handed Michael the booklet. "You can keep this copy of the fentanyl course outline. If it doesn't provide enough details for your article, you're welcome to sit in on our program orientation seminars. We hold them in the conference room. The next one is in three weeks. You can ask the presenter any questions you want."

We'd be back in Montreal by then, but Michael accepted the book. "Thanks."

"How successful is your job placement rate for applicants?" I asked Jerry.

He avoided looking at me. "I haven't reviewed the latest stats yet."

"Don't you keep any stats on the number of people who got a job after they took a course?"

"Well..." Jerry's focus darted to papers in a tray on his desk. "We do, but I don't have access to them right now. However, rest assured. After the thousands of dollars the government spends on rehab treatments, we take all the necessary steps to ensure candidates find good jobs."

I ignored his ambiguity. "What steps do you take?" I felt Michael's eyes on me. Had I come across as too assertive? Had my questions crossed into forbidden territory?

Jerry pointed a thumb in my direction and grinned at

Michael. "I understand why you bring your research assistant along to these meetings. She doesn't look the part, but she sure asks the tough questions." He chuckled.

I didn't share his humor. It was condescending, to say the least.

Michael stepped in. "Megan beat me to it. I would have asked you the same questions."

I waited for an answer from Jerry.

"The steps we take..." Jerry drummed his fingers on the desk. "First, we do rigorous testing after each course presentation. The applicant has to pass a test or else it's back to the drawing board. Second, we assist in the job application process where we teach the ins and outs of job hunting. Third, we instruct candidates how to conduct themselves during job interviews and how to follow up on interviews they get. There are other parts to the program, but it gives you a general idea." He waved the topic away.

I wasn't finished. It surprised me that all those efforts would be undertaken ad hoc with no measurement of actual results. I rephrased my original question. "How do you measure the success of your program?"

"If the applicant lands a job, it's a success." Jerry beamed.

"Do you ever get complaints from employers who hire them?" I kept my expression blank, wondering how many times he would avoid answering this particular question.

He glanced away. More tapping of fingers. "None that I'm aware of."

"One other question," Michael said. "Would you happen to know Becca Landry?"

Momentarily stunned, Jerry replied, "Yes. In fact, I do. She used to work here. Why do you ask?"

"Megan and I are staying at the Dorfin Hotel this weekend. There was a mix-up in the rooms when we checked in. We walked in and found her body."

"Hell." Jerry passed a shaky hand through his hair. "We got

the news this morning when the police arrived. What a terrible tragedy. My staff is in total shock."

"We're sorry for your loss," I said.

"Thank you."

Michael leaned forward. "Do you know how she died?"

"No idea. The police are investigating. I don't know any more than that. In fact, they're here talking to my staff right now."

"Had Becca been working here long?"

"About a year." Sweat glistened on his forehead. "She was a hard worker. She put in long hours—especially last week. We had deadlines to meet."

"When was the last time you saw her?"

"Last Friday." Jerry's eyes grew moist and he sniffed. "I felt she deserved extra compensation for the tough week she had. That afternoon, I gave her a keycard to the Dorfin Hotel for a weekend stay."

So that's how Becca paid for the hotel room!

I could hardly contain my surprise. "That was a generous gesture on your part."

Jerry smiled. "It was worth it. You should have seen Becca. She was so happy. I'll never forget it."

"I never thought of gifting a hotel room," I said, prodding him to say more about it. "It's an interesting idea."

"Actually, I re-gifted it." He briefly looked down as if he were embarrassed. "An associate had given it to me, but I couldn't use it. I was going to a baseball game with friends Friday night and had other plans for the weekend."

I would have given anything to know the identity of Jerry's associate. Was this person the regular occupant of room 634?

Michael shuffled his feet. A sign of uneasiness? Did it mean I shouldn't pursue the subject any further?

To my surprise, Jerry said, "You know, I did it from the heart. I thought Becca would appreciate a weekend break. And now..." He sniffed. "Sorry. I still can't get over what happened."

"Her unexpected death must have devastated her family," I said.

"She was married and had two small kids."

Michael stepped back into the conversation. "We saw her husband on the news. He told reporters he thought Becca was murdered."

Jerry lowered his voice. "Becca had a rough time with her husband after he returned from a tour of duty some months back." He scratched his ear. "The war can play havoc with your head. Those military types can fly off the handle without notice. Some of them suffer trauma in the field and come back with psychological problems."

"You think her husband..." I paused, leaving the sentence open-ended on purpose.

Jerry held up his hands, palms out. "Oh, don't get me wrong. I'm sure they had a good marriage. I wouldn't have given her a keycard to the hotel if their marriage was on the rocks, now would I?" He reinforced his argument with a one-shoulder shrug.

"I suppose not," I said.

Jerry gazed at Michael and me. "How did you know Becca worked here?"

Michael kept a straight face. "Someone at the hotel knew her."

Jerry bought it. "Becca knew lots of people. She was a hell of a good employee too. We're going to miss her."

"Excuse me, Mr. Leduc," a male voice called out behind us.

We turned to see Detective Grist standing in the doorway.

"Is your tech employee on his way here?" he asked.

"I sent him a text message," Jerry said. "What I mentioned earlier about privacy concerns—"

"Send him another message," Grist said. "I don't have all day." He turned and hurried away.

Jerry tensed up, then asked us, "Any other questions?"

"No," Michael said. "Thank you for your time."

We'd stepped into the corridor when Jerry called out, "Oh, Michael, before I forget…"

Whatever Jerry wanted to tell Michael, I hadn't a clue. Since he hadn't called me back, I kept on moving along the corridor.

Detective Grist was standing in front of the closed office several feet ahead of me, a folded paper in his hand. "Hey, Megan. Funny how we keep running into each other, isn't it?" He smiled.

I ignored his comment and peeked into the office.

Becca Landry's nameplate was partially covered by a pot of leafy flowers on her desk, which explained why I hadn't noticed it when I'd walked by earlier. Several framed certificates graced the back wall, most of them bearing official-looking seals and signatures. "So this is where Becca Landry used to work."

"Yes." The detective changed the subject. "This can't be much fun for you."

"What?"

"You know. Following Michael around while he researches boring information for his article and other stuff."

"I find it interesting."

Amusement danced in the detective's eyes. "If you were my girl, I'd be showing you the sites around town."

I'm nobody's *girl*. "There'll be time for visiting later." I kept my tone even.

He chuckled softly. "I can see that some things never change with Michael."

"Oh?"

"Work comes first. Women come a distant second. It accounts for the instability in his relationships with women all these years."

I stared hard at him. "That's because he hadn't found the right one until he met me."

Before the detective could answer, a young man wearing jeans and a T-shirt walked up to us.

"Detective, I can get into Becca's computer for you now, but my boss says some of the information is hands-off because of privacy concerns."

"Don't worry. This warrant covers any concerns he might have." The detective tapped the sheet of paper in his hands. "Excuse me, Megan." He followed the employee into Becca's office and shut the door.

Grist wanted access to her computer. Something was up.

12

Michael steered the car out of the parking lot and drove along Wellington Street. We passed the Gothic-style structure of the Parliament Buildings nestled atop the Hill overlooking the Ottawa River.

Crowds of visitors ambled across the expansive front lawn, snapping photos of themselves in front of the Centennial Flame and sculptures and monuments dotting the grounds. The crowds were small compared to Canada Day celebrations on July 1st when a hundred thousand people gathered on the Hill to watch the entertainment and fireworks show.

From an earlier visit to Ottawa, I recalled that the front lawn of Parliament Hill was also the setting of the daily Changing of the Guard ceremony. A glance at my watch told me we'd missed it by half an hour. Damn!

Were we ever going to find time to visit the sites in this city?

It was clear that Detective Grist's negative comments about Michael were still nagging at me. I had to find a way to move past them.

As if he'd read my mind, Michael said, "How about taking a short drive along the Rideau Canal? We have some free time."

The lush scenery would definitely help clear my mind of negativity. "Sure."

I'd researched the Rideau Canal for my client's project and discovered that it was the largest naturally frozen skating rink in the world. Called the Skateway when frozen, it hosted tens of thousands of visitors every day from January to March. Stands along the skating path served hot soup, hot chocolate, and BeaverTails—a deep-fried, cinnamon and sugar pastry that was also available in the ByWard Market year-round.

Only now, the route bordering the canal was active with walkers, runners, and cyclists who moved along its picturesque green banks and boaters who traveled in its waters. The landscape soothed away recent worries, if only for a little while.

Michael's voice broke the silence. "Megan, you haven't said more than a few words since we left Jerry's office. What's wrong?"

I recalled Detective Grist's comments about Michael, but I refused to entertain them further. Instead I said, "The detective gained access to Becca's computer. What do you make of it?"

"I have a hunch he suspects foul play. I'll contact Becca's husband later. He might know more."

"What did Jerry want?"

"He offered me tickets to an all-star baseball game the city is hosting soon."

"That was considerate of him. Did you accept them?"

"No, we'll be back home in Montreal by then," Michael said. "We'll do something special to celebrate Canada's 150th birthday there. Okay?" He squeezed my arm.

"Okay. Sure." Other things were weighing me down—like Jerry's attitude toward me. "Did you notice how Jerry avoided— or rather—had a hard time answering some of my questions? Either he's not on top of things or someone else is managing the day-to-day operations over there."

"Yeah, I noticed that too. Don't take it personally. Could be the guy's overwhelmed by what happened to Becca. I can't blame him. Our timing was off."

Okay. Maybe I was wrong about Jerry. Yet his comments about Frank bothered me. "I didn't like the way he implied Frank was aggressive. I wonder how well he knows him."

"I'd bet that Becca confided in Jerry about her problems—financial and otherwise," Michael said. "From what Frank told us, all she did was work. She didn't have many friends or a social life to speak of."

"So you think Jerry felt sorry for Becca and gave her the keycard."

"Yeah. He was just trying to help."

I let it go at that.

Michael checked the time. "How about grabbing a bite to eat? I'm meeting with a paramedic this afternoon to discuss the local drug scene. It's his day off. Then I'm sitting down with a colleague at a local radio station."

"I'm getting together with my friend, Tasha Dufour."

"The events planner you told me about?"

"Right. She sits on the planning committee for some of Canada's 150th anniversary events."

"Sounds like fun," Michael said.

"Partly," I said. "I'm interviewing her for that project I'm ghostwriting for a client."

"Oh. The usual dry stuff." He grimaced in jest.

"Compared to your thrilling job, of course," I teased him.

I'd tried to find a more interesting career choice years ago, but none offered a decent salary *and* the option to work off-site. So I did the next best thing. I built up a steady flow of freelance ghostwriting jobs and worked from the comfort and predictability of my home office. As far as I was concerned, I was my own boss and had cornered the best of both worlds.

It wasn't as if Michael and I didn't work well together, though. We made the best investigative team. I helped him with research and tagged along when he interviewed witnesses. Our jaunts took on a darker tone when unexpected trouble crossed our path. The possibility of not seeing tomorrow on several endeavors had given me heart palpitations, but we managed to get out of a bind every time. Joining Michael on his ventures added spark to my otherwise dull career. Best of all, it enabled me to pull him from the edge of danger in case he took one risk too many.

Michael's voice broke into my thoughts. "I promise we'll do something exciting tonight, Megan."

"Okay." I smiled at him, knowing he meant it.

Michael was full of surprises, and now he had intrigued me once again. What was he planning for us tonight?

Tasha Dufour was smart and business-savvy and used her solid five-foot-ten height to advantage. In heels and upscale clothes, she projected a confident image and a formidable challenge to anyone who might doubt her abilities. As an events planner in Ottawa, she'd established a small but successful operation by getting to know the right people in the right places. And the nation's capital knew no bounds in this respect.

I'd first met Tasha in Montreal when I was looking for an events planner for my wedding to Tom years ago. We connected and became good friends. Although the wedding proceeded without a hitch, my marriage to Tom went in the opposite direction.

Tasha had moved to Ottawa in the interim, and we'd kept in touch. She was ecstatic when I called her a week ago to let her know I'd be visiting. I was eager to see her this afternoon and get the inside scoop on local events for my ghostwriting project.

Tasha chose Zoe's Lounge in the Fairmont Chateau Laurier for our meeting place. Its stylish décor, comfy chairs, and elegant chandeliers made it a popular dining spot and the perfect setting for high tea.

She removed her wide-brimmed hat with a navy trim and placed it on an empty chair between us.

"I love your hat," I said.

"Thanks. I have six of them—one for every color scheme." She laughed.

"You know, I've never been to high tea before."

"I'm sure you'll love it. Did you know the British working class regarded high tea as their evening supper?"

"No, I didn't know that."

"In fact," Tasha said, raising a manicured forefinger in the air, "high tea developed into an afternoon tea tradition only in America."

I preferred coffee, but when offered a choice of flavored teas that included raspberry and orange, it was too good to pass up. Not to mention how much I drooled over the three-tiered tray of fancy petit fours, savory tarts, and biscuits.

After champagne was served, Tasha and I chatted about everything from fashion trends to the latest movies. It was as if time had stood still and we were back in the past, planning my wedding and choosing all the niceties. Our chat extended to our jobs, and we laughed at our foibles and those of our clients.

At one point, Tasha sipped her champagne and grew quiet. Clouds blew across her usual upbeat personality, and she appeared lost in somber thoughts.

"Is everything okay at home, Tasha?"

She jolted back to the moment, flashing a smile. "Never been better. Jack is doing great. The twins are fine. Want to see a picture I took last week?" She scrolled through the photos on her phone and picked one. "Here are my little cuties." She held out the phone so I could see the photo.

Her three-year-old twin girls were dressed in blue-and-white striped tops, matching shorts, and tiny sailor hats.

"They're adorable," I said.

She placed her phone on the table. "I wish I could spend

more time with them, but my days are pretty full right now." She morphed into a downhearted state again.

"Tasha, we've known each other a long time. I can tell when something's bothering you. Care to share?"

She sighed, then reached for her phone again. "I received disturbing news this week. A woman I met in the course of my work passed away. We'd become good friends. She was about our age."

I touched her arm. "I'm so sorry."

"You know how it is when you meet someone and it just clicks, right?"

I smiled. "Yes."

"Of course, you do." Her smile faded in the next moment. "Well, when I met this woman, we hit it off right away. Here's a photo of her." She showed it to me.

I couldn't believe it. I recognized the woman, except her hair was shorter. "I think I know this woman. What's her name?"

"Becca Landry."

13

———————

I briefed Tasha on the discovery of Becca's body in our hotel room, sparing her the gruesome details.

She reached for her glass of champagne and drank it down. "Oh, my God. Oh, my God." She poured more champagne into our glasses, spilling a few drops on the tablecloth. "They say it's a small world, but this is incredible."

I digressed to what I hoped was a more cheerful time in her memory. "Tell me how you met Becca."

Tasha leaned back in her chair. "It was about a year ago. A company called Looking Ahead asked me to bid on a project. That's where Becca worked."

I refrained from mentioning that Michael and I had met with Jerry Leduc earlier. I didn't want to put a bias on Tasha's recounting of events.

Tasha smiled. "I won the project. They asked me to plan a fundraising event. That's how I met Becca. Her husband Frank was in the military and stationed overseas at the time. She had two small kids and a mother-in-law to take care of. She didn't have much of a social life, but we got together for a drink once in a while to blow off steam."

"Was she loyal?"

"Oh, yes, but that didn't stop men from approaching her. Whenever we went out for a quick drink after work, men flirted with us but especially with Becca. She had a certain vulnerability that men go for. You know, that wispy, slender blonde type. If Becca were here, she would wag a finger at me for saying that about her." Her eyes welled up, and she hid her sadness with a laugh.

"When did you last see her?"

"Last Friday afternoon at about two o'clock. I was sitting in the lobby of Looking Ahead, waiting to meet with Jerry Leduc to discuss another project. I heard shouting from the offices at the other end of the corridor. Becca and a man were having an argument. Becca shouted, 'I can't do it anymore, Jerry!' before she stormed past me and out the door."

"What did you do?"

"I wanted to run after her but couldn't. Jerry had come to get me for our meeting."

"Did he say anything about the argument?"

Tasha nodded. "Behind closed doors, he told me that Becca was overworked and needed a break. He was embarrassed and came up with that excuse."

"You didn't believe him?"

"On the contrary, I did. Becca had told me she put in long hours during the week and worked weekends too."

I remembered how upset Frank had been about Becca's overtime schedule too. "Did she complain about it often?"

"Every time we met. She groaned about the extra hours she had to work without pay, how her boss was often late in paying her and the other employees, the responsibility of signing legal documents..."

"Legal documents?"

Tasha shrugged. "She probably meant standard documents for the company."

It was odd that Frank hadn't mentioned Becca was a signing officer at the firm. Maybe he didn't know.

Tasha moved on. "Anyway, Becca said her situation was a catch-22. She wanted to quit her job but was afraid to leave because it would be difficult to find another job. Naturally, I didn't think she should up and quit. On the other hand, with her educational credentials, believe me, she'd have no problem finding a job that paid better."

I recalled Becca's framed certificates in her office. And yet Frank had downplayed her qualifications the last time we met with him. Had Becca taken the courses and not told him?

I had to get the facts straight. "So it all came down to Becca complaining about long hours and lousy pay."

"I don't know how much Becca earned, only that she wasn't happy working there. If you ask me, Jerry was a tad selfish."

"What do you mean?"

"To make up for his tardiness, he paid his employees in cash to save them a trip to the bank. Did he lose any sleep over the anxiety he created among them? I doubt it."

I couldn't reveal the vast sum we'd noticed in Becca's purse, so I tried a workaround. "I hope she wasn't paid on a monthly schedule. That's a long time between pays."

"She was paid every two weeks. It doesn't matter. Even if the paycheck is only a few days late, it makes a difference when you have bills to pay."

"That's true." I did the math. Frank had confided that Becca earned twenty-five thousand dollars a year. The net income after taxes and other deductions for two weeks would have come to about eight hundred dollars at most. Far from the two thousand dollars found in her purse.

Had Becca lied to Frank about her salary? If not, where did the extra cash in her purse come from? Frank had access to the bank account he shared with Becca, and it didn't sound as if they were swimming in money. I made a mental note to discuss this with Michael.

Tasha took a sip from her glass. "Anyway, Jerry's a penny pincher when it comes to money. Would you believe he didn't even install a security alarm system in the office? Sure, this is Ottawa where the crime rate is insignificant compared to other cities, but Becca didn't feel safe working late hours alone. It can get pretty scary on the streets after business hours. They roll up the sidewalks here after five o'clock—figuratively speaking, of course."

"The streets were filled with people till late hours in the ByWard Market the other night," I said.

"It's tourist season, that's why, though I heard the planning bureaucrats are trying to liven things up. They'll have it all figured out in fifty years." She giggled.

I sipped some champagne. "Do I detect a hint of cynicism?"

"With flying colors. After dealing with so many VIPs, I learned who to trust and who not to. I particularly avoid the 'bureaucratized ambiguity' of dealing with politicians in this town. They pay well, but their projects drag on forever." She rolled her eyes. "As for scrooges like Jerry, I keep after them with a stick until they pay me. A verbal stick, of course. I bombard them with emails until they give up."

Our server came by and asked if we needed anything. Tasha and I said no at the same time and she left.

"Oh, by the way." Tasha reached for her handbag. "I have tickets for you and Michael to a fundraising event on Friday. Jerry's organization is featured. The aim is to raise funds for addiction treatment. It's one of several events I organized for him." She handed them to me. "You'll have an opportunity to socialize with the who's who of local government and non-governmental groups. There'll be food and drinks, and I'll be there, so your evening won't be a complete write-off." She laughed.

"Thanks. It should be interesting." I happily stuffed them in my handbag. I had yet another question about Becca and guided the conversation back to her. "I meant to ask you earlier.

Did you get a chance to speak with Becca after she rushed out of Jerry's office Friday afternoon?"

She smiled. "Yes, she called me. It was almost five-thirty. I remember because I'd just called home to make sure my nanny had dinner in the oven. Becca told me she'd gone back to the office and worked things out with Jerry. He gave her a keycard for a free weekend at the Dorfin Hotel. She said it would be like a date with her husband. She was on her way there, and then she and Frank were supposed to go out for dinner and spend the weekend at the hotel. She sounded so happy." Her smile vanished and she looked down.

"What?"

She fingered her napkin. "I was thinking. It's possible the pressure Becca felt had nothing to do with her workload."

"What are you saying?"

Tasha poured the last of the champagne into our glasses. "Maybe she was having an affair with someone at the office. Maybe another man was the pressure she was referring to."

"Were there any signs?"

"Only the late hours she worked." She paused. "Of course, most women don't go looking for affairs, do they? They just happen. With her husband overseas, maybe Becca got lonely."

The business card from the clinic that had slipped out of Becca's purse came to mind. If she were having an affair, could she have been pregnant with another man's child? Did she visit the clinic because she was planning to have an abortion? I needed to visit that clinic as soon as possible.

Tasha winced, misinterpreting my moment of concentration. "Oh, my God. You must think I'm a horrid person. Forget what I said about Becca having an affair." She waved a hand in front of her face. "It was spiteful. I'm just looking for someone to blame for her death. Believe me, she wasn't the type to have an affair. She was loyal, whether her husband was here or in another country. She loved her family and would never do anything to hurt them."

The pendulum had swung the other way.

If so, maybe the "important news" Becca wanted to share with Frank on the weekend was her pregnancy. It was a joy that she hoped would revive their marriage.

I needed to confirm something else first. "Would you say that Becca and Frank had a good marriage?"

Tasha hesitated. "Well... Sort of."

"You don't sound too sure."

She sighed. "Like I said, Becca and I became instant friends. She confided in me about three things that disturbed me. First, Frank left the military after he suffered a leg injury while on active duty. He couldn't get a job when he returned home. Second, he had mood swings and complained about the pain in his leg. Third, his medication was expensive. I'm convinced it all put a strain on her marriage and added to the pressures at work."

"It could explain why she wanted to hang on to her job."

"Yes. It also explains the long hours she worked too. Her job provided stability and security—something she didn't have at home."

"Because Frank was unemployed?"

"Not exactly." Tasha bit her lip. "I hate to say this, but sometimes I wondered if she felt safe with Frank."

Goosebumps rose along my arms. "What are you getting at?"

"They argued a lot. From what Becca told me, she suspected Frank suffered from PTSD—Post Traumatic Stress Disorder. He refused to see a doctor. All he wanted were the painkillers."

"Wait. Go back to what you said earlier about Becca not feeling safe at home. How do you know this?"

"Becca met me for lunch one day. She had bruises on her arms. When I asked her how she got them, she said she tripped over her kid's toy on the stairs one night and slammed into the railing." She blinked hard. "What a tale!"

"You didn't believe her?"

"No way. She never had bruises when Frank was overseas, only after he returned. It happened more than once. How would *you* explain it?"

I couldn't. I offered her a shrug, reached for the silver teapot the server had just set down, and filled our cups with raspberry-flavored tea. I'd need to ask Frank about those bruises.

Tasha continued her rant. "And where was Frank anyway? Why wasn't he in the hotel room with Becca?"

I sipped my tea and said nothing. Michael and I had promised Frank we'd keep our meeting with him confidential.

"Another thing." She raised a forefinger in the air. "Let's suppose that Frank refused to go to the hotel to meet her that Friday evening. Do you know what Becca would have done?"

"Tell me."

"She would have gone back home to be with her family. She wouldn't have stayed at the hotel." Her eyes filled with tears, and she reached for a tissue in her handbag. "Sorry, Megan. I'm so angry. I can't believe Becca is gone." She sniffed. "I think I've had too much champagne. I always get emotional when I have a glass or two." She dabbed at her tears.

I touched her arm. "Don't be so hard on yourself, Tasha. You're allowed to grieve. You lost a close friend."

She patted my hand. "I'm so happy you're here. How much longer do you expect to be in Ottawa?"

"A few more days."

Tasha asked, "Is Michael still working as an investigative reporter?"

"Yes. Why?"

"I'll be direct. Do you think you could persuade him to investigate what happened to Becca?"

"Isn't the police—"

"Forget the police. They don't know Becca the way I did." She lowered her voice. "Her death wasn't an accident, like they probably suspect it was. She didn't take her life either. She would never do that to her family." She dropped a sugar cube in her tea.

Tasha was the second person to maintain that Becca hadn't killed herself.

"Please, Megan, would you ask Michael to investigate her death for me?"

Michael and I were already investigating Becca's death on Frank's behalf—albeit by our own choice. Tasha's official request might drag us in deeper than we ventured to go.

In any case, I couldn't let her down. "I'll ask him."

"Thank you." She put a hand on her chest, then whispered, "Believe me when I say this. Becca was murdered."

14

———

By the time the taxi dropped me off at our hotel, Michael had returned from his meeting with the paramedics. He greeted me at the entrance to our suite with a kiss. "I was starting to miss you."

I smiled. "That's a good sign."

He chuckled. "Did you have fun at high tea?"

"Yes." After I'd spent two hours with Tasha, my brain was overflowing with information about Becca, not to mention the remaining effects of two glasses of champagne. "I have so much to tell you. I don't know where to begin."

"Let's sit down. I didn't know if you were going to have lunch or not, so I ordered a few munchies from room service in case."

I followed him into the living room.

Tins of assorted nuts, mini bags of chips, a bowl of popcorn, cans of pop, and a bottle of White Zinfandel dotted the coffee table. All his favorite junk foods.

"Oh. We ate already. You go ahead, Michael."

"How about a glass of wine? It's one of your preferred white wines, and I don't want to drink alone."

"Okay."

He filled our glasses and handed me one, then sat on the sofa next to me. "What did you want to tell me?"

I briefed him on my conversation with Tasha, including her suspicions that Frank had physically abused Becca. "Tasha believes that Becca couldn't possibly have killed herself. She wants to know if you can pursue an investigation on her behalf."

Michael leaned forward and clasped his hands. "We already agreed to investigate on Frank's behalf. So far, we've gathered information that just doesn't add up. Too many loose ends. If we take into account what Tasha said, Becca's death is getting more and more suspicious."

"So can I tell Tasha that we'll investigate for her?"

"You bet. She might even be able to help us fill in some gaps."

I mentioned the tickets to the fundraising event Tasha had given me.

He smiled. "There you go. She's helping us already."

"How?"

"I'll bet a lot of fat cats are on the guest list. Tongues wag after a few drinks. You never know what might come out of their mouths. Maybe inside gossip about hotel room 634 or Becca, or even chatter about the lack of government financing for drug abuse control. If they believe they're among supportive colleagues, bureaucrats tend to talk."

"I'm looking forward to it then. Oh, one more thing. Tasha mentioned Becca's educational credentials and how she wouldn't have a problem finding another job. Those credentials could be the certificates I saw hanging in Becca's office."

"It's weird that Frank didn't mention them. Maybe Becca was holding back on him."

"Maybe." I changed the subject. "How did your meeting go with the paramedics?"

He sat back in the sofa, stretched his arm behind me. "They

have a local plan to increase the number of supervised injection consumption sites for drug users. The sites help prevent the spread of diseases like HIV."

"Not to mention drug overdose deaths."

"Right. They shared stats on the opioid overdose cases here. Gruesome numbers. A lot of emergency calls involved teens. If the government doesn't crack down on illegal drug traffickers, more young people are going to die."

"I feel sorry for the parents of kids who get addicted to drugs. Can they get treatment for them?"

"Demand for treatment centers and programs for addicts far exceeds the ability to provide the services. The bottom line: Treatment is available in private facilities—if you can afford it."

"It sounds as if law enforcement and the government are losing control in the war against drug abuse."

Michael nodded. "Paramedics treat overdose victims every day. They encounter the same symptoms we saw the other night in the ByWard Market. Sometimes coma or even death."

I shivered. "What a horrible way to die. The ByWard Market is such a beautiful part of the city. Drug-trafficking incidents can taint public perception of the area."

"Insiders know it's a hotspot for drug dealers. Tourists, not so much."

"It's a good thing Jerry's organization offers courses on the subject."

He picked up the booklet Jerry had given him and flipped through the pages. "For what it's worth."

"What do you mean?"

"Slim pickings. There's not much in here."

"He said it was an outline. Maybe the class sessions expand on it."

"It's possible." He put it aside. "About fentanyl... I suspect that Becca might have bought Frank's fentanyl pills in the ByWard Market after work, then driven to the hotel from her office."

"The timing is wrong," I pointed out. "Tasha told me Becca called her at about five-thirty from work. She was on her way to the hotel."

"Right. Her check-in time at the hotel was five forty-five." Michael grew pensive. I could almost see the wheels turning in his mind as he figured out the timing.

I did the math too. "Becca couldn't possibly have driven around town in that short a time—especially not during the Friday afternoon rush hour. She must have driven straight to the hotel from work."

He reached for his glass of wine. "Ten minutes tops. Add another five or so for parking and check-in at the front desk."

Realization sunk in. "Either Becca got the fentanyl pills where she worked, or she got them from someone at the hotel. Do you think her death had anything to do with a drug deal gone bad?"

"I doubt it. The packet in her purse was a small purchase." His eyes lit up. "Megan, you realize we've just narrowed down the geographic scope of our potential drug dealers. Now we have to do the same for Becca's killer."

I took a sip of my wine. "You're not going to like this, but from what Tasha told me, we have to add Frank Landry to our list of suspects."

Michael's forehead creased. "You're right. I don't like it."

"Why not?"

"You already know the answer. It's too easy to assume the spouse did it."

We'd been down that road before and in a scenario that fell much closer to home. I set aside my objections—for now. "Do you have anyone else in mind?"

"Whoever had access to Becca's hotel room last Friday."

"We've already reviewed the activity list for her room. Only the housekeeping staff and Dylan, the service attendant, entered the room before Becca did."

"Right. Using their master keycards."

"Let's not forget the regular occupant—whoever he is. He had ongoing access to the room with his own keycard."

Michael sipped more wine. "There was no entry recorded in the room after Becca arrived at quarter to six."

"Who said after? He could have walked in at any time." I caught myself. "Forget it. There was no sign of a struggle, and the preliminary autopsy report stated she died from an opioid overdose."

"You're forgetting someone else."

"Who?"

"Jerry Leduc."

"Jerry gave Becca his keycard," I said. "How would he have entered her hotel room?"

"I didn't imply that he did. Who's to say he didn't knock at her door after she checked in?" Michael wiggled an eyebrow.

"He told us he had other plans for the weekend." I stopped. "Oh, I get it. You think he's her mystery lover?"

He placed his glass on the coffee table. "Could be. Maybe he lied about his weekend plans."

"No way. They had a huge argument at work that Friday before Becca walked out."

"She might have pretended she couldn't stand the guy. Their argument could have been an act. According to Tasha, Becca went back to the office afterward. Patched things up with Jerry."

"It doesn't mean they were having an affair. Tasha believes Becca was loyal to her husband."

Michael persisted. "If she was having an affair, she wouldn't go around broadcasting it. Not even to her best friend."

He was right. I didn't find out about my husband's affairs until after he was dead.

Yet when I tried to visualize Becca and Jerry together... "I don't see it. Jerry wasn't her type." Another name on a business card in Becca's purse flashed through my mind. "What about Randall Thorne?"

"What about him?"

"Don't you think it's odd that Becca would have his business card in her purse?"

"Not really. His foundation funnels sponsorship funds to Jerry's group. The men have a business connection, and from the looks of it, a very respectful relationship."

"I still find it odd that Randall's card would be in her purse."

"Here's a thought," Michael said. "Maybe Becca interacted often with him or his office staff and kept his number handy."

"She could have added him to her phone contacts. Besides, Randall said he didn't even know her. Do you think he was lying?"

"Question is: Even if Becca knew Randall, would she have let him into her hotel room while dressed in sexy lingerie?"

"Probably not, unless—"

"He was a client of another sort. Possibly one from her escort services days. Maybe an additional source of revenue?" He threw me me a questioning glance.

The idea suddenly sounded ridiculous. "I doubt it. Besides, we're grasping at straws. Tasha is convinced that Becca was a loyal wife, and I trust her judgment."

"Let's keep Randall in mind anyway. I agree there's a reason Becca had his business card close at hand. He might be worth exploring further."

I pursued my original line of thought. "Someone else could have knocked at her door, though."

"Go for it."

"Frank Landry."

Michael tensed up. "Hold on. I see where you're going with this now. We've circled back to Frank. Blame the husband, why don't we?"

"Frank admitted he was at the hotel."

"He waited in the lobby. He didn't say he'd gone up to Becca's room. Hell, he didn't even know her room number." He let his hands fall to his thighs with a thud.

"You don't have to get upset about it."

"I'm not upset." His flushed face said otherwise.

"Yes, you are."

"Okay. Time out." He leaned back, joined his hands behind his head, and stared at the ceiling. "Let's approach this another way. We know Becca died from opioids. The question is: How did it happen?"

"Unless we gain access to the final autopsy results, we're wasting our time trying to figure it out."

"You're right. Let's go get some answers." He stood up and pocketed his phone.

I rose to my feet. "Where are we going?"

"Let's have another chat with Frank."

15

————

Activity in the hotel lobby had diminished. People had either left to see the sites in town or were in their rooms, getting ready for dinner.

Michael slowed down on our way out. "Hold on, Megan. Eric's at the front desk."

"So?"

"He's alone."

"What about it?"

"Remember how nervous he was when Andy was around? Let's go talk to him." He darted toward the front desk.

I hurried to catch up to him.

"Hi, Eric," Michael said. "Working alone today?"

Eric smirked. "Yeah. It's Andy's day off. What can I do for you?"

"I wanted to ask you a few questions about what happened Friday night."

Eric spoke in a hushed voice. "Management said we're not allowed to talk to anyone about...the incident."

"It's actually not about the incident."

"It isn't?"

"No. It's about a man who was waiting in the lobby last Friday at around six o'clock. Maybe you noticed him. He walks with a slight limp."

Awareness flashed in Eric's eyes. "Yeah, I remember him. A guy with a crew cut wearing a sports jacket." He stopped. "I can't talk about it."

"Why not?"

He leaned in and kept his voice low. "He's connected to the incident."

"How?"

"He was the dead woman's husband."

"You're kidding me, right?"

Eric shook his head. "No, I'm serious. He gave Andy a really hard time."

"Tell me what happened. I'll make it worth your while." Michael slipped a folded fifty-dollar bill across the counter.

Eric hesitated, then casually slipped the money into his pocket. He whispered, "You didn't hear this from me. Okay?"

"Okay," Michael said.

"Sure," I said.

Eric went on. "The man had been hanging around the lobby for a while—at least half an hour. He came up to the desk to speak with Andy. He said his wife was supposed to meet him in the lobby at six o'clock, but she never showed up. He asked Andy to tell him what room his wife was in."

Michael asked, "Did Andy give him the room number?"

"No."

"Why not?"

"Andy explained that guest records were confidential. That was when the trouble began."

"What trouble?"

"The man kept repeating that he was her husband, that he had every right to see his wife, yadda, yadda, yadda. Andy and I were busy with other customers, but he insisted that we serve him right away. He was getting real angry about it."

"Why didn't you call the room and speak with his wife?" I asked him.

"I'm getting to that part." Eric cast a glance around to make sure no one was within hearing range. "Andy scanned the customer list and couldn't find anything in the wife's name. He didn't tell her husband because we're not allowed to reveal those details. It's all about privacy."

I whispered, "What happened afterward?"

"Andy sent him up to the tenth floor," Eric said. "There's a hotel lounge up there."

"Why would he send him there?"

"To get rid of him. The man was acting like a lunatic. Andy suggested his wife might be there."

Michael asked, "Did you see her husband take the elevator up to the lounge?"

Eric hastily said, "I didn't check. I was too busy. Sorry, that's all I got." He moved away to serve another customer.

"Slight change of plans," Michael said to me as we hurried away from the front desk. "Let's go up to the lounge. If Frank spent some time there before he drove out of the garage, maybe the bar attendant can narrow the time frame for us."

"So that we can eliminate Frank as a suspect?" Sarcasm tinged my words. "How convenient."

"Why are you so doubtful? Eric just confirmed that Frank didn't know Becca's room number."

"Maybe Frank pretended he didn't know."

"That's what we're going to find out eventually. Not every lead is direct, but we have to start somewhere."

I let it go at that. "Any news from your tech friend about the hotel surveillance video?"

"No, he hasn't contacted me yet."

"That piece of evidence could either refute Frank's alibi or set him free."

"I'll take my chances and bet it's the latter." Michael's tone was confident.

"What if Frank lied to us?"

"About what?" He hit the up button for the elevator.

"He insinuated he'd stayed in the lobby the whole time he was here. If he went up to the lounge, why didn't he tell us? He's not supposed to drink alcohol anyway, so why go up to the lounge?"

"There are lots of unanswered questions and just as many theories. We have to be patient and take one step at a time."

"Okay, but Frank is still a potential suspect on my list."

"We'll need to see the hotel video footage before we can jump to any conclusions, Megan."

Touché.

~

Late afternoon patrons had already gathered in the lounge. Chatter and laughter competed against the sound of clinking glasses and pulsating music.

Uh-oh.

Roger was sitting at the bar, chatting up a young woman in a business suit. He noticed me and waved.

I gave him a quick nod, then said to Michael, "Do you think we'll get lucky?"

"Only one way to find out." He raised a hand and caught the attention of the bar attendant.

Wearing the standard black bowtie and vest over a white shirt and black pants, the attendant strode up to us. "What can I get you?"

"Were you working here Friday evening?" Michael asked.

He passed a hand along his trimmed beard. "Nope. That was Dylan."

"Is he working tonight?"

"Nope. He's off today. He'll be here tomorrow night."

The strong scent of beer floated my way.

I turned to see Roger at my side.

"Hey there, honey. We meet again." A guffaw trailed his introduction.

"Hi." I looked past him to an empty seat at the bar. The woman in the business suit had left. Michael was still chatting with the bar attendant. Damn! "What happened to your lady friend, Roger?"

He jerked a thumb over his shoulder. "Oh, she had to go to some political event in town."

"That's too bad."

"Yeah." He smiled. "Hey, you never did tell me what floor you were staying on." The beer sloshed in the glass mug he was holding. "We could get together some time."

Didn't this guy ever get the message?

I changed the subject. "Did you ever hear back from the police about your witness statement?"

"No." Roger squinted. "Why would they follow up with me? I told them everything I knew."

"It's common knowledge that a critical witness to a crime sometimes turns out to be a prime suspect."

"Hey, I'm no suspect."

"The police don't know that for sure. That's why they keep close tabs on all witnesses."

Roger's eyes bulged. "You mean, like tracking us?"

"Yes. They could be working undercover, and you wouldn't even know it."

Unease spread across his face. "Oh, I never thought of that." He warily scanned the lounge.

Michael arrived at my side. "Hi, Roger."

Roger mumbled something, then drifted toward the bar.

"What's wrong with him?" Michael asked.

"I gave him a dose of his own medicine." I laughed. "What took you so long?"

"The attendant was telling me how some guests openly ask for illegal drugs at the bar."

"What do they tell the guests?"

"That the hotel doesn't do drugs."

"Do you think someone's lying?"

"Tell me about it."

The sun's early evening rays filtered through the curtains as Frank's mother eased herself into an armchair in the living room. She leaned back against a fluffy cushion and smiled at Michael and me.

"We were never formally introduced. My name is Agnes. I was thinking about calling you, but you popped up instead. I'm so glad you did." Her voice was weary, as if the events of the past week had drained her of energy. "The kids are upstairs watching TV, so we're free to talk."

"Where's Frank?" Michael asked her.

Worry lines deepened across her forehead. "He's gone. He packed a bag late last night and left without a word."

"Do you know where he went?"

She wrung her hands. "No. I heard the front door slam shut at about midnight. I looked out the bedroom window and saw Frank drive off."

"What does he drive?"

"A red pickup truck."

"Did anything happen recently that could have caused him to leave?" I asked her.

Agnes sighed. "The police were here last night. Detective Grist and a uniformed officer." Her bottom lip trembled. "They dropped off Becca's purse and other personal belongings from the hotel. They also had the toxicology reports. The results were incomplete, but Detective Grist said they found an excessive level of a certain drug in Becca's system."

"Did they mention the name of the drug?" Michael asked.

"I'm not familiar with it. They called it the date rape drug. It had fancy initials."

"GHB?"

"I'm sorry, I don't remember."

Michael leaned forward. "Did the police say anything else?"

"Oh, yes." She tightened her lips in annoyance. "They put Frank through the same drill as the first time they came here. Questions about his prescribed fentanyl usage, his trip to town to meet Becca at the hotel... On and on it went."

"Did the detective mention if foul play might be involved in Becca's death?"

"He didn't say as much, but I could tell by the look on Frank's face that something wasn't right. He doesn't trust cops —especially Detective Grist. He thinks he has tunnel vision and is looking for a reason to blame him for Becca's death."

Michael said nothing. This latest development complicated things.

"Frank stayed strong until the police left here," Agnes said. "Then he broke down and cried like a baby. We all did. Becca's death has been hard on the kids." She took a tissue from her pocket and blew her nose.

"Is there any way we can contact Frank?" I asked her.

"Oh. I almost forgot." She reached for a phone on the corner table. "Frank left his phone behind. I don't know if he forgot it or left it here on purpose. It's of no use to me. Frank calls us on the landline in the house. I expect we'll hear from him when he gets his life together." She handed me Frank's phone. "In the meantime, you might find something on it that could lead to his whereabouts."

I slipped it into my handbag. We'd access Frank's contact list as part of our investigation as soon as we left.

I recalled Tasha's claim that Frank might have physically abused Becca and carefully chose my words. "The last time we met with Frank, he confided that he and Becca had gone through a rough period in their marriage after he completed his tour of duty. Did he ever lose patience with Becca?"

"No," Agnes said. "Frank and Becca had words once in a

while. Most couples do. I think their arguments had to do with Becca's long work hours. Nothing more."

I rephrased my question. "Was Frank ever aggressive?"

She stared at me, now fully aware of what I was implying. "If you mean physically aggressive, the answer is no. My son is a good person. He's not much of a talker—never was. He keeps to himself a lot. He might not say it, but he loved Becca with all his heart and would never hurt her." Tears threatened to spill from her eyes. "I never asked for much in my life, but now I'm pleading with you. Please find evidence to prove my son is innocent."

As soon as we entered our suite, Michael accessed Frank's phone. He patiently scrolled through his contacts, calls, and messages. "The only outgoing calls are to Becca's cell phone. Dozens of them."

"It confirms that she didn't pick up," I said. "Or couldn't."

"Right. She'd probably passed out from the date rape drug." He tapped a key. "Photos of Becca and the kids at home, the playground... Family stuff." He tapped more keys. "Oh. There's one more outgoing call here to a place called Onward Home."

I reached for my phone and searched online for a local business by that name. "It's a medical establishment that treats drug abusers. Do you think Frank was a patient there?"

"Maybe. We know he depended on fentanyl for pain relief."

"So he needed intervention for drug dependency? He was an addict?"

"Anything's possible."

16

Detective Grist held a press conference Tuesday morning regarding his investigation into Becca Landry's death. In keeping with our morning routine, Michael and I sat on the living room sofa to view the coverage on TV.

As soon as it was over, the media ran a clip of a reporter trying to interview Jerry Leduc. Jerry refused to comment and scurried into his office building.

"It's interesting how the media latched onto Jerry," I said. "It just proves how small Ottawa is, in spite of the million or so people who live in this town. You can't do anything without word spreading about it."

"Yeah. Jerry looked exasperated." Michael turned off the TV with a click. "So am I, but for a different reason."

"What do you mean?"

"I'm not buying what Grist said."

"Which part?"

"All of it. Grist is turning this investigation into a witch-hunt. Just because Frank disappeared doesn't make him guilty."

"It certainly doesn't help his situation." I strolled over to the window and let my eyes settle on the low-rise buildings across the street. "It makes Frank look as if he's guilty and definitely as if he's running away."

"I've worked with Grist before," Michael said. "He's a damn good cop. I don't understand why he launched a countrywide search for Frank based on zero evidence."

"Maybe he feels pressured to solve the case. Look at the factors. Becca was a mother of two, married to a military man, and found dead in a hotel. It draws public sympathy."

"Whatever the reason is, Grist is trying too hard. Telling the public that Frank is considered a person of interest in an alleged suspicious death doesn't cut it. Anyone can interpret the dubious meaning behind those words."

I returned to the sofa and sat next to him. "Maybe he has more evidence than we do."

"Could be. Based on our meeting with Agnes, something tells me it might have something to do with the drugs in Becca's autopsy report. Regardless, Grist needs motive and opportunity to pin her murder on Frank. In my book, there's an obvious lack of both."

"What's our next move?"

Michael took a moment to reflect. "We'll go up to the hotel lounge tonight and talk to Dylan. If we're lucky, we'll get evidence to prove Frank didn't go anywhere near Becca's room."

"What about the hotel video from your tech friend?"

"He sent me a text message earlier. I should receive a copy of the video today. For Frank's sake, let's hope it fills in all the time gaps."

"Detective Grist must have viewed it by now. If he suspected Frank, wouldn't he have brought him in for questioning days ago?"

Michael had another theory. "It's possible the information on the video was incomplete, or it didn't capture the evidence he was looking for."

The earlier TV clip of Jerry Leduc played in my mind. With

good reason. I'd forgotten to tell Michael about the certificates I'd seen under Jerry's desk. I briefed him now.

"It might not mean anything," I said, "but the sample letter on the box cover had an official-looking gold seal on it, like the kind you see on diplomas or certificates."

"Under his desk? That's a strange place to store them."

"He probably issues certificates to graduates who complete courses through his firm."

"Makes sense." Michael sat back, joined his hands behind his head, and stared at a point in the distance. "Okay, let's concentrate on the scene of the crime—the hotel room—and recap what we've learned so far."

I listened, ready to contribute my share.

He began. "For starters, there were no signs of a struggle in Becca's hotel room and no sign that she had been physically assaulted. There was no record that anyone entered the hotel room after she arrived. At least not with a keycard."

It was my turn. "We have a new development: the GHB—or date rape drug. How did it end up in Becca's system?"

"If it was in liquid form, GHB takes effect within minutes. It would be hard to detect in a dark drink."

"So we have to assume the GHB was in the carafe of wine."

Michael nodded. "Becca could have taken a few sips to calm her nerves before she called Frank and invited him up."

"Would it have been enough to kill her?"

"We don't know what the GHB dosage was. In some cases, it can be fatal. More so if combined with alcohol."

"We can assume two more things," I said. "First, according to Frank, the fentanyl pills in Becca's purse were for his use. Second, someone dropped the GHB into the carafe of wine that was delivered to Becca's hotel room, which means it was intended for her." I extended that thought. "Or for Frank."

Perception flickered in Michael's eyes. "You might be onto something. I never thought of Frank as a potential target."

"I was being cynical."

"Let's keep an open mind. We still have to go through the motions and prove his innocence."

Michael was right. We had no proof that Frank had killed his wife. I had to keep an open mind and focus only on tangible evidence. If anything, I owed it to my friend Tasha to uncover the truth behind Becca's death.

He continued. "Certain individuals connected to Becca and room 634 might turn out to be prime suspects." He raised a finger as he named each one. "The regular occupant of the room—whoever he is. Jerry, who argued with Becca, then gave her a free weekend pass. Randall, because of his business card in her purse. Dylan, the attendant who delivered the wine."

"Jerry and Randall said they weren't in town that evening," I pointed out. "Neither was the regular occupant. I thought we'd already eliminated them."

"People lie. Jerry and Randall might have wanted to get rid of Becca for reasons that we haven't yet discovered. Until we learn the identity of the regular occupant of room 634, we shouldn't eliminate him either."

"So what's next on the agenda?"

He stood up. "Dylan won't be staffing the bar in the lounge until tonight. Let's go visit Onward Home. We'll drop by to see Jerry at work afterward. If Grist asked the tech guy to access Becca's computer there, I'd like to find out why. It could hold a clue to her death."

"What makes you think Jerry will confide in us?"

"If he cared at all about Becca, he'll want to find out how she died."

I grabbed my handbag. "Why would he need us to do that? Detective Grist is leading the investigation."

"Jerry didn't seem as welcoming to him. And vice versa."

"Maybe Jerry has more to hide than just a box of certificates under his desk."

17

Something past its due date came to mind as I shook hands with Ed Finch. His sunken eyes and pallid skin reinforced that impression, as did an oversized suit that would have hung better on a metal clothes hanger. He motioned for Michael and me to sit in the vinyl chairs facing his desk while he lowered himself into a threadbare armchair across from us.

"I've been medical director at Onward Home for the past two decades." Ed puckered his thin lips. "We can't boast a one hundred percent success rate, but we've come close. We give newfound hope to people who've lost sight of it." He grinned, revealing smoke-stained teeth.

I diverted my attention to the wall behind him where framed diplomas hung. Two diplomas were from well-known Canadian universities. Other certificates were from institutions like the National Academy of Higher Education and the Distance Learning Quality Assurance Agency. I didn't recognize these names, but each certificate included an official-looking gold or red seal like the ones hanging on the walls in the outer corridor.

Ed went on. "Michael, I understand you're looking for information about our programs for an article you're writing on drug rehabilitation."

"That's right," Michael said. "To begin with, I'd like to know how the application system works."

Ed tapped a pile of papers with his bony fingers. "Many of these applications are from drug users who feel isolated but are determined to kick the habit and make a fresh start. Therapists, physicians, and other consultants that work with us are tasked to review and assess each application. Since we're financially limited and depend on government handouts, we only accept a certain number of applicants for our programs. It's a difficult choice."

"What happens to the applicants that you have to reject?" I asked him.

Ed raised his lean shoulders in a shrug. "They sometimes reapply at a later date." He moved on to another subject. "Michael, you mentioned on the phone that you and Megan were also researching the fentanyl crisis."

"Yes, that's how your company name came up," Michael said, twisting the truth a little. "I'm hoping that my article will help to promote institutions like yours, which might encourage more government funding for your cause."

"I like the sound of that." Ed joined his fingers. "How can I help your research?"

"Give me examples of the types of people that you accept as candidates."

"We have a wide range. It spans from homeless people to professionals who are trying to beat the drug habit."

"I have a friend who completed a tour of duty months ago. He was injured and is trying to get off a fentanyl habit. Would he qualify for your program?"

"Definitely," Ed said. "Since the sponsored funds we receive are limited, we like to accept candidates who are already covered in part by government health programs. Military personnel would qualify in that respect."

"Are your courses held in this office?" I asked him.

"Oh, no." Ed chuckled. "They're only offered online."

"How do homeless people access them?"

"Some shelters provide these services, though I can't name them off the top of my head." He fingered another stack of paper on his desk, making a feeble attempt at pretending to look for a list. "In fact, we receive very few applications from homeless people. With the increasing number of fentanyl overdoses lately, many street users don't live to see tomorrow."

I shuddered inwardly. It was a morbid statement coming from someone who'd expressed hope moments earlier.

Michael stepped back into the conversation. "We recently interviewed Jerry Leduc of Looking Forward."

The director's eyes reflected interest. "Oh, I know Jerry very well. His staff produces excellent online courses for the candidates accepted into our program. As long as his group keeps offering such fine programs, we'll keep bringing in the applicants for them. Small world, isn't it?" Another chuckle.

"Yeah." Michael pressed his lips together, as if to hold back a reproach on the inadequate course outline in Jerry's booklet. "One last question. Do you know the success rate of candidates who have taken the program and obtained jobs?"

Ed's expression turned wistful. "No, I'm afraid this is the extent of our role in the process. You can always ask Jerry. I believe he keeps records on that."

A scowl formed on Jerry Leduc's face. "I'm sorry, I can only give you a few minutes of my time." He sat down behind his desk. "As you can see, we're in full promotion mode."

His desk was littered with publicity paraphernalia begging for organization. The chaos extended to items piled on a table by the window, bookcase shelves, and the floor. I had half a mind to get up and put the place in order.

Instead I made a pretense of placing my handbag on the floor so I could peek under Jerry's desk. Yes, the box containing certificates with gold seals was still there. Only now a second box sat beside it. It contained certificates with red seals.

"I'll be direct with you," Michael said. "We're here to talk to you about Becca."

Jerry's tone soured. "I've had a tough time escaping the media this week. I can't afford more bad news coverage."

"We're here on behalf of Becca's family. They're looking for answers."

"In case you haven't noticed, the police are investigating her death." Jerry's retort was snappy—a striking change from our previous visit.

Michael was adamant. "Journalistic privilege. That's what I'm offering you. Whatever you say stays in this room."

Jerry heaved a sigh of exasperation. "I have nothing to say to you—least of all about Becca. Like everyone else here, I'm trying to get over the shock of her death."

The tug of war between them was going nowhere fast. "You had a heated argument with Becca the day she died," I blurted.

"Who told you that?"

"It's not important. Tell us about the argument."

Jerry forced a smile. "It was no big deal. Becca complained about working overtime. She said she was suffering from burnout. She wanted to spend more time with her family."

"That's not the version we heard," I said. "Apparently you had quite the argument, raised voices and all. Becca was very upset when she left your office."

Jerry raised his hands. "Enough. I take the entire blame for her burnout, okay? I tried to make it up to her. Like I told you, I gave her a free weekend at the Dorfin Hotel."

"Yeah, and it didn't cost you a damn cent," Michael said.

Veins throbbed in Jerry's neck. "Don't you think I regret giving Becca that weekend pass? It damn well escalated the situation between her and her husband."

"What are you getting at?"

"Her husband's military tour of duty was cut short because of a leg injury last year. From what Becca told me, he had PTSD and gave her a rough time at home."

"So?"

"He met her at the hotel. If you ask me, something must have happened between them. He probably went into a rage and killed her." He smirked.

"Your assumptions are unfounded," Michael said. "The cops haven't labeled Becca's death as a murder."

"Not yet." Jerry glanced at his watch.

I pressed on. "Is that why Detective Grist accessed Becca's computer? He's investigating a lead to a potential murderer?"

Through clenched teeth, Jerry said, "I never said that. Don't put words in my mouth. I don't know why the hell he accessed her computer files."

"We thought you cared about Becca."

He slammed a hand on his desk. "Of course I did!"

"Then help us get answers for her family."

In a Jekyll and Hyde twist, Jerry calmed down and moved on to another topic. "I thought you came to town to cover the fentanyl crisis." He fixed his gaze on Michael.

"We did," Michael said.

"Then you should have enough stories to work on without stirring up a hornet's nest."

"I'm not stirring up—"

"Drugs on the street. Deaths by fentanyl overdose. Those are the real stories. The actual predicaments happening in this city and across the country."

"That's exactly what we're doing."

Jerry stood up. "I'm sorry, but that's all the time I have for you. If you're as smart as I think you are, Michael, you'll stop digging into Becca's life and save yourself a load of opposition."

"Opposition?" Michael echoed as we rose to our feet. "From whom?"

"Let me spell it out for you." Jerry lifted his chin. "In this town, agencies and partner businesses like mine survive on public funding and handouts from government. We can't afford any negative backlash that the media doles out."

"Is that a threat?"

"No." Jerry's eyes narrowed. "It's a friendly word of advice. Take it."

18

———————

After our meeting with Jerry, Michael headed out for a jog. He hadn't perceived Jerry's "words of advice" as anything less than a threat to his journalistic freedom. He told me he needed to calm down in case he'd give vent to his frustrations. Jogging provided a release.

I took action of another sort.

After I dropped Michael off near the Parliament Buildings on Wellington Street, I drove to Many Choices clinic in town. When I'd called the other day to make an appointment, the receptionist had confirmed that it was a pro-choice clinic—one of several such legal clinics in the city.

I had to answer preliminary questions over the phone and give my name, age, and marital status. Since I didn't want to reveal my true identity, I gave her fake information. As for my alleged pregnancy, I lied and told her I was six weeks along.

My first meeting was scheduled with a counselor named Renata. She was qualified—the receptionist had assured me—to answer any questions I had.

~

Renata's soothing voice and welcoming attitude put me at ease the moment she greeted me in the reception area. But no matter how amicable she was, I doubted she'd easily share information about Becca with a perfect stranger. I'd have to wing it and give it my best shot.

We settled on the white couch in Renata's closed office. Vibrant photos of young babies hung on the pristine white wall opposite us. Colorful caps and bonnets framed their cute faces and would trigger any woman's maternal instincts. A sudden and inexplicable twinge of remorse shot through me as I played along and pretended to be pregnant.

"Our group is all about offering choices." Renata's voice was as smooth as the strand of white pearls around her neck. "After considering the options, women have three choices. Abort their pregnancy, offer their baby up for adoption, or keep their baby." Her smile deepened the wrinkles around her eyes and mouth. "Have you made your decision yet?"

"Uh...no," I said, surprised by the question. "That's why I came here. I'm looking for answers."

"That's perfectly normal. Let's discuss your options one at a time. If you decide to have an abortion, you need to consider the physical and emotional consequences of terminating a pregnancy."

"Consequences?"

"Yes, dear. There are risks involved. Serious risks."

"Can you be specific?"

"Women who have had abortions are unable to conceive later on. Many have suffered depression and anxiety and have even become addicted to drugs."

Her reply stunned me. I had researched the topic and knew that her claims weren't the norm.

"Let me show you something." She reached over and plucked a pile of photos that were placed face down on the small table before us. "I must warn you. These photos were taken at various stages of pregnancy." She gave me a wary look before turning them over.

There were three photos of aborted babies at intervals of six, eight, and ten weeks. The form of their minuscule bodies was easily identifiable.

"Oh, hell." Bile rose in my throat and I covered my mouth.

"I know exactly how you feel," Renata said. "Most women have the same reaction when they see the termination of these poor innocent babies." She gathered the photos and placed them face down on the table.

I tried to compose myself, though wiping the photos from my memory banks would be a more difficult—if not impossible—undertaking.

"As for adoption," she said, "and from my experience here, many women have regretted their decision to hand over their newborn child to a stranger. They had to seek psychiatric help to overcome their guilt." She sighed and placed a hand over her heart. "You'll have to forgive me. I don't know how any mother can give away their own child."

"Surrogate mothers do it all the time," I said. "Mothers who don't have the money to provide a good home for their kids might—"

"Megan, please stop." Renata eyed me up and down. "You're not a surrogate mother, are you?"

"No."

"Fine then. You're obviously a smart woman. I don't need to explain the third option to you. Keeping your baby to full term is by far the best choice. You and your partner will enjoy much happiness as you watch your baby develop into a fine adult."

Talk about making false medical claims. This establishment professed to be a pro-choice clinic whose consultants offered unbiased information and services. It was far from it. I would have left right then, but I hadn't asked about Becca yet.

I grabbed the opportunity when Renata asked, "By the way, how did you find out about our clinic?"

"Through a friend of a friend. Someone gave me a name as a reference and told me the woman had come here to discuss her pregnancy. Her name is Becca Landry. Do you know her?"

Renata's demeanor changed. "You're not working with the police, are you?"

My pulse raced. "The police? No. Why would you think that?"

She brought her voice down to a whisper. "We don't usually discuss other clients. It's just that… Well, a police detective was in here asking about her the other day. Surely you've heard the news about her death last week." She waited for a reaction.

"No, I was out of town," I lied, then added, "Like I said, I didn't know her personally."

Sadness clouded her eyes. "I met with her last week. She was such a lovely girl. I told her that keeping the baby would help ease the situation at home. Now I'll never know what she decided to do."

"The situation at home?"

"Oh." Renata put a hand to her mouth. "I've said too much already." She changed the subject. "So, Megan. Have I helped you make your decision?"

"Yes, you have." I stood up. "I'm keeping the baby."

I thanked her and hurried out, gulping a breath of fresh air. I wasn't even pregnant, yet guilt and shame filtered through me.

I'd tried to put myself in Becca's place and sought answers from a clinic that was supposed to inform pregnant women about their choices. Instead I'd sat through a lecture from a biased consultant with anti-abortion views who steered me toward what she believed my choice should be.

I made my way to the parking lot in a state of confusion. Maybe Becca had felt the same way after her meeting here last week. Above all, I was disappointed that, in spite of my consultation with Renata, I'd made no progress in finding out what Becca had decided to do about her pregnancy.

Had she decided to keep the baby in spite of Frank's PTSD

and physical problems, not to mention their tight financial situation?

Or had she planned to meet with Frank at the hotel to tell him she was getting an abortion?

Was Becca's strained relationship with Frank the "situation at home" that Renata had referred to?

If so, was Tasha right about Frank? Was he capable of harming Becca? Or worse?

19

———

Back in our hotel suite, I told Michael about my experience at the women's clinic. "I felt horrible. After my meeting, I couldn't wait to get out of there. I can't possibly imagine how it would feel to have to make a decision like that."

"I hope you never have to," Michael said. "I'd love to see you pregnant with our child one day." He smiled at me.

I said nothing and sipped some wine.

He took my hand in his. "I'm not pressuring you, Megan. You know that my feelings on the subject haven't changed."

The sincerity in his voice was hard to miss. "I know, but we've been through this before. Many times. I'm not ready to remarry, let alone have a baby."

His tone grew softer. "If memory serves me right, wanting a baby was on your wish list once upon a time."

"Yes, I wanted to have children when I was married to Tom, but things have changed since then."

Michael stared at me. "How am I supposed to interpret that?"

"Don't take it personally. It's *my* problem. It's something I have to work out at my end, although I have to admit..."

"What?"

I smiled. "Those cute baby pictures at the clinic stirred up something inside me."

"Aha! There it is. Your maternal instinct is alive and well." Michael smiled.

"I'm only human, you know. It's easy to imagine how torn Becca must have felt after she left the clinic."

"Maybe she decided to keep the baby and wanted to share the news with Frank."

I offered another viewpoint. "Or their financial situation was so stressful that she wanted to discuss it with him before making a decision about the baby."

"I guess we'll never know."

The Tuesday evening crowd at the hotel lounge was as noisy as the last time Michael and I had stopped by. The dance floor vibrated with the beat of the music, supporting gyrating patrons in business attire or casual wear. Though the area around the bar was filled to capacity with thirsty patrons, Michael managed to get a seat for me.

Dylan was one of three bar attendants on duty. As Michael caught his eye, he waved in our direction. He finished pouring a beer for a customer before walking up to us. "Good to see you both again. What can I do for you?"

"Two glasses of sparkling water, please," Michael said.

Dylan soon returned and set the glasses down. He leaned in and kept his voice low. "About that wine delivery, it was on the regular occupant's tab."

"So he ordered it."

"Not necessarily."

"What does that mean?"

"Like I told you before, either the regular occupant or the weekend guest could have ordered it."

"I need more information." Michael discreetly slid a folded fifty-dollar bill toward Dylan who made it disappear in the next moment. "Were you working here last Friday night?"

"I was. From six to midnight."

"Did you notice a guy, mid-forties, military haircut? He was looking for his wife."

Dylan nodded. "Yeah, I remember him. He sat at the bar. Must have been early evening between six and seven. The place was bouncing with the office crowd."

"Can you narrow the time frame?"

Dylan shot a glance at the patrons along the bar. He nodded and raised a forefinger in someone's direction, then said to Michael, "My shift here started at six o'clock—right after my room service delivery run. I'd say it was between six-fifteen to six-thirty."

"What exactly did the guy say to you?" Michael asked.

"Like you said. That he was looking for his wife and that she was a guest at the hotel. He showed me a photo on his phone. She was pretty hot." He grinned.

"Did you see her in the lounge last Friday?"

Dylan grabbed a cloth and wiped the countertop. "No."

"She was staying in room 634," I said to him.

"Oh." Dylan blinked. "The same woman I—" He stopped.

"You what?" I asked him.

He wiped the same spot on the counter. "I delivered wine to her room late Friday afternoon."

"You have a good memory."

"Not really. The cops asked for my service delivery records when they questioned me."

"Had you seen her in the hotel earlier?" Michael asked.

Dylan gave his head a quick shake. "I was too busy with room service to notice anyone."

"How long did her husband stay in the lounge?"

"About fifteen minutes. Maybe more. I didn't keep tabs."

"Do you know where he went afterward?"

"No."

"Did he have anything to drink?"

"Just sparkling water," Dylan said. "No hard stuff. He ordered two bottles and drank them down real fast. That's all I know." He slithered away to serve another customer.

Michael dimmed the lights in our penthouse suite. The starry view through the expansive window gave me the impression the sky was going to suck me into it at any moment.

He handed me a glass of red wine. "I thought we could use something a little stronger than sparkling water. I uncorked a bottle of red wine from a supply in the complimentary bar." He sat next to me on the sofa. "Cheers."

I took the glass and clinked his. "Cheers." I took a sip. "I wish we had more to cheer about."

"Why so glum? We're making progress with Frank's alibi. We confirmed he took Andy's suggestion and visited the hotel lounge Friday night."

"He didn't find Becca there, but he stayed and drank two bottles of water in about fifteen minutes. Weird."

"It's not that weird," Michael said. "Increased thirst can be a side effect of fentanyl."

"That explains it." I drank more wine. "I don't understand why Frank would even think that Becca had gone to the lounge alone."

"I guess he wanted to explore every option."

"Talk about trust. Why didn't Frank tell us he'd gone up to the lounge to begin with?"

"He probably thought it wasn't important."

"What? Not important? If I were Frank, I'd be trying my hardest to prove my alibi. For all we know, he could have spent the rest of the time looking for Becca in the hotel before he drove out of the parking."

"Once we get the video, we'll be able to fill in the gaps." Michael checked the time. "I'll give my tech friend a call."

"At this late hour?"

"It's only ten o'clock. He works later than this." He reached for his phone, hit the speed dial, and waited. "He's not picking up." He left a short message.

"Maybe he went out with his friends or something."

"No way. The guy has no social life. It's all about working in the tech world out of his tiny apartment. The only person he sees once a week is his mother. She's in a retirement home."

"If you like, we can have him over for dinner one night," I said.

Michael laughed. "Good try, Megan. You'll do anything to find out who he is, won't you?"

I laughed. "Not at all. I was just trying to be sociable."

He leaned over and kissed me on the lips. "Thanks." As he looked out the window, the moonlight cast shadows over his face. "Time's running out. We have to broaden our investigation to other suspects."

"We've been through this before. What good does it do?"

He drank some wine. "We must have missed something. A tiny tipoff. Let's go over the suspect list again."

I studied the process from another angle. "I think we should work backwards."

Michael squinted. "Backwards? What do you mean?"

"When I'm editing a piece, I read a line of text backwards to pick up typos. We can work backwards by figuring out who was the last person to see Becca alive."

He set his glass on the coffee table. "Okay. Let's do it. We know that the last person to access Becca's room before she arrived was Dylan. Let's assume he dropped the GHB into her wine carafe. Question is, why would he want to kill Becca? Or Frank, for that matter?"

"Maybe he's working for someone else."

"We could say that about any suspect."

As hard as I tried, I couldn't let go of my initial suspicions. "What about Frank?"

Michael replied with a familiar refrain. "We'll need to see the hotel video to confirm his comings and goings. Question is, why would Frank drug his wife? With his military background, he'd have chosen a less obvious place and method to get rid of her if he wanted. Right?"

"I see your point. On the other hand, he could easily justify his presence at the hotel. Becca invited him there."

He rubbed his brow. "Sorry, it doesn't sit right with me."

I wasn't giving up entirely. "We'll wait for the video then."

"Let's stay on track. What about Jerry?"

"What about him?"

"His working relationship with Becca."

"Tasha thinks the friction between them was about Becca working long hours and disliking aspects of her job, like signing documents."

"What documents?" Michael retrieved his glass a little too quickly. Droplets of red wine spilled onto the table surface. He dabbed the spill with a napkin.

"She didn't know."

"Okay. Next we have Randall Thorne."

"Randall and Jerry have a business connection," I said, "but Randall claimed he didn't know Becca."

"Which leaves us with the regular occupant of room 634." Michael sipped his wine. "Whoever he is, he probably didn't even know Becca was staying the weekend in his room."

"Let's keep this unknown variable in mind anyway."

"No problem."

My next words revealed what the deep recesses of my mind had already dared to imagine. "Becca loved her family, but what if she was depressed from the pressure she felt at home and at work? What if she had a death wish and did herself in? We still don't know if she swallowed any of the fentanyl pills she had in her purse."

"True. The final autopsy results will determine that."

"Detective Grist will see them before we do. We'll have to rely on Frank to share the results with us. That is, if he ever shows up."

"I should call Grist."

"And tell him what?"

"Enough to show that we're doing our part. Maybe he'll share what he found in Becca's computer at work."

I was still seething from Detective Grist's rude remarks about Michael. "Don't you think he would have contacted you by now?"

As silence fell between us, I pondered our findings. The dilemma was in determining which suspect had the most to gain from Becca's death. To do that, we needed a lot more pieces to the puzzle.

Michael bolted upright, almost spilling his wine again. "Damn!"

I jumped. "What?"

"We've overlooked an important lead. Becca's contact for the fentanyl pills. After Jerry threatened me to stop investigating Becca's case, I was convinced he had something to hide, but..."

"But?"

"Jerry is disorganized. I was thinking of someone else."

"Dylan?"

"You bet," Michael said. "He's the only one who had access to Becca's hotel room. He seems to know a lot about the drug trade. He could have purchased the fentanyl pills and dropped them off in her hotel room before she arrived."

"Isn't that risky?"

"Taking chances is what pumps the adrenaline in these guys."

"What about payment? How could Becca have paid him?"

"She could have paid him in cash when she got to the hotel. According to the timeline, she might have even bumped into him when he was working the delivery run on her floor."

"If you're right, Dylan lied to us. What's our next move?"

"We need to prove that he's involved in the drug trade. The only way to do that is to follow him."

"When?"

"Tonight."

20

George Street in the ByWard Market was empty, except for a drunken straggler winding his way along the sidewalk steps ahead of us. His presence and the shuffle of his footsteps seemed out of place, as if someone had forgotten to tell him the street party had ended a while ago.

Michael and I had tailed Dylan from the hotel after his bar shift had ended at midnight. Donned in dark clothes, we blended easily into the late-night crowds sifting through the market's popular streets dotted with pubs and eateries.

We followed Dylan to the edge of the Market where the crowds were thinner. The locals knew better than to wander into an area that turned seedy in the wee hours of the morning. Our suspicions about the purpose behind Dylan's trip to this part of town were slowly taking shape.

I whispered to Michael, "What if he sees us?"

"Don't worry," he said. "We're at least twenty feet behind him."

Just then Dylan glanced over his shoulder.

Michael swiftly moved in front of me and kissed me, hiding our faces from him.

"That was fast thinking," I said.

He took my hand in his. "Let's cross the street. The parked cars over there will give us more cover."

We watched as Dylan stopped in front of The Salvation Army building. He approached a couple of men wearing dark hoodies—likely contacts in this black-market drug trafficking section of town.

Michael and I crouched behind a parked car and watched Dylan through the windows. If our instincts were right, this meeting could reveal that Dylan was Becca's potential supplier of fentanyl.

The next step would prove more challenging. We needed to find evidence that he'd dropped GHB or a similar drug into the wine carafe in her hotel room.

How we could possibly substantiate these theories was beyond me, but Michael assured me we'd succeed.

"I need to video this." Michael dug out his phone and raised it slightly above the hood of the car. His determination reflected the courage and conviction that were consistent traits in his investigative work.

I often wished I were as brave as he was.

Fat chance. I had a hard enough time trying to stop my teeth from clattering right now, let alone keep my knees from knocking. The warm summer breeze did nothing to assuage either.

A guttural shout reached us from across the street.

One of the men pulled out a gun!

"Damn you, you're nothing but a thief." The man pointed his gun at Dylan.

Dylan held his hands up. "Whoa, Shank. I paid you guys the same amount for this stuff the last time."

"Like hell you did. You're trying to screw me."

"No. You just don't remember."

"Playing games with me, eh?" Shank raised his voice. "Well, the price just doubled."

"Forget it," Dylan said. "I'll get my stuff elsewhere." He put his hands down and turned to walk away.

"Don't you dare walk away." The man waived his gun. "We have a deal."

Dylan shouted over his shoulder, "To hell with your deal. I'll tell everybody what a scammer you are."

Two gunshots pierced the air and echoed in my ears.

Shank and his accomplice scrambled into a car and sped off, tires screeching.

I gaped in horror as Dylan staggered, then crumbled to the ground.

21

I instinctively reached for Michael, but he wasn't there.

He was racing across the street toward Dylan!

I dashed after him.

Dylan was curled up in a fetal position on the sidewalk. He was gasping for air as blood seeped through his white shirt and flowed into the shadows.

I swiftly retrieved my phone and dialed 911, then gave the dispatcher the required details.

Michael got to his knees. "Dylan, I need names. Who shot you?" He leaned over to hear his faint response.

Out of nowhere, someone handed Michael a towel. He grabbed it and applied pressure to Dylan's wound.

A small crowd had gathered around us.

One woman peered over, covered her mouth, and hurried away.

Two young girls drew near and gaped at the sight. "What happened?" one of them asked.

A man in a T-shirt replied, "The guy got shot. I saw the whole thing. I got the getaway car on the camera right here." He held up his phone as if it were a trophy.

Michael kept talking to Dylan and leaning closer to hear his replies.

Sirens wailed in the distance.

The nightmare wasn't over yet.

~

The paramedics transferred Dylan onto a stretcher and lifted him into the ambulance. A queasy feeling had hit my stomach earlier when I overheard one attendant tell the other that Dylan had become non-responsive.

Police officers spread through the crowd and took witness statements. By now, the red and blue lights atop their cruisers had attracted a sizable group of curious bystanders, including the media. Photos of the crime scene and the people in it would hit the social media circuit any moment now.

One officer thanked Michael for coming to Dylan's aid and told him, "Ottawa had a record number of shootings this year. Half of them involved street gangs. You're lucky you didn't get killed."

Michael confided he was working on an investigative article about drug abuse. "I didn't expect to see this kind of interaction firsthand."

"This is a lucrative spot for drug dealers," the officer said. "And a common one for gang shootings. Gangs fight to protect their drug turf, no matter what. The incidents of violence have increased in the last decade. It's all about control."

After the police gave us permission to leave, we returned to our hotel suite. It was two o'clock in the morning.

We took turns taking a shower. Michael went first, washing off traces of Dylan's blood from his hands and arms. After the horrible night we'd had, I couldn't fathom getting into bed without removing the grimy feeling the incident had left on me.

I snuggled next to Michael in bed afterward. "I hope Dylan is going to make it."

"Yeah. Me too."

"Getting shot is a tough price to pay for backing out of a drug deal."

"I'll say." The darkness accentuated Michael's sigh. "Dylan didn't look too good. The paramedics said his blood pressure was extremely low. We'll call the hospital tomorrow to see how his emergency surgery went."

"We hardly know Dylan, but I feel so awful about what happened to him. I wonder if he has family here."

"I gave them our room number and my phone number as references—in case."

"This whole drug business is so demoralizing. It claims so many victims."

Michael pulled me closer. "Guys like Dylan are always looking for ways to make a quick buck. They get involved in illegal stuff way over their heads."

"Do you think he knew he was dealing with a dangerous street gang?"

"I'm not sure, but anyone who deals in drugs is opening the door to danger."

"It's almost impossible to trust anyone these days, isn't it?"

Michael put a finger under my chin. "Oh, I don't know about that. I trust *you*." He kissed me.

"It works both ways." I kissed him back.

His phone rang. He reached for it in the dark and answered. "Yes, it's Michael. I see. Thanks for calling." He placed the phone on the nightstand.

"What is it?"

"Bad news." He hesitated. "Dylan didn't make it."

"Oh, no!"

"The poor guy never regained consciousness."

My memory replayed the scene on the sidewalk: Michael leaning over Dylan, straining to hear what he was saying. "With everything that happened, I forgot to ask you. Did Dylan give you the names of the shooter and his friend?"

"Yeah," Michael said. "I passed the info to the cops."

"Did you get a chance to ask Dylan if he'd drugged the wine in Becca's hotel room?"

"I did."

"And?

"He said no, he didn't."

"Did you ask him anything else?"

"I asked if he'd sold fentanyl pills to anyone last Friday. He said yes but passed out before I could get a name."

"Do you believe him about the wine?"

"If he sensed he only had seconds to live, he was probably telling the truth."

Shivers ran up my spine. "Then Becca's killer is still out there."

22

Michael's phone woke us up the next morning.

Who would dare disturb us at the crack of dawn?

I peered thought the darkness at my phone on the night-stand. It was ten o'clock in the morning!

The bedroom had blackout curtains from ceiling to floor, and Michael had drawn them shut last night—or rather earlier this morning—before we went to bed.

"We'll be there in an hour," Michael said to the caller. "See you soon."

I threw off the bedcovers and sat up. "What? Where are we going? Who were you talking to?"

Michael got out of bed. "Agnes. She asked us to go over."

"Did she hear from Frank?"

"No. She's worried about a man in a suit who came looking for him this morning. She wants to talk to us but not over the phone. She has information that could help our investigation."

"I need coffee."

"We'll get coffee and some French croissants before we head out."

~

Agnes perched on the edge of the sofa and leaned over to hand us a business card. "This is the man I was telling you about, Michael. He said he worked for the government and wanted to speak with Frank."

Michael read the information on the business card. "Leo Gagnon, Canadian Anti-Fraud Center."

"Anti-Fraud Center?" I repeated.

"It's an agency managed by the RCMP," he said. "The CAFC collects information and criminal intelligence on matters like telemarketing fraud, Internet fraud, and ID theft complaints." He handed the card back to Agnes. "Did the agent say why he wanted to talk to Frank?"

"No," Agnes said. "Only that Frank should call him when he gets back." She heaved a sigh. "Frank has never been gone this long without contacting me and the kids. Something is wrong. Call it mother's intuition, but I can feel it."

"He's probably working out a few things," Michael said. "Losing Becca was tough on him."

"Yes, it was." Agnes grew pensive. "I have something else to show you. I'll be right back." She stepped out of the room and returned moments later with a portfolio. "Frank is handling Becca's estate and came across an insurance policy not long ago." She pulled out a document and placed the portfolio on the coffee table. "This is a policy for Becca from Journey Life. It's for a million dollars."

"A million dollars?" I repeated.

Agnes nodded. "You heard me right."

"Did Frank know about this insurance policy?" Michael asked her.

"No. He was so surprised when he found it. I mean, who goes out and gets a policy for a million dollars a year before they die?" She flipped to an inside page. "Here it is in black and white."

Sure enough, the details were clearly indicated. I scanned the page and noted that Frank was the sole beneficiary. "Why didn't you show us this the last time we were here?"

"Frank was worried about how it would look. It's so much money." She sunk into the armchair.

"Not to be intrusive," Michael said, "but would you know if Frank has a similar policy?"

"Oh, my goodness, no. He could never afford expensive coverage like this. He's in a group insurance policy offered through the military."

"Did Frank question the policy at all?" I asked her.

"You mean, did he think it was fake?" Agnes let out a small laugh. "We both did at first, until Frank called the company and it turned out to be legitimate."

"Did he file a claim yet?"

"Yes, he drove over there to sign documents. They told him they needed to wait for the police report to ensure Becca's death wasn't ruled as a suicide before they could disburse the funds." She looked perplexed. "Why Becca took out such a generous policy is a mystery. I can only hope things get sorted out soon. The insurance money would take a lot of pressure off Frank."

A recent memory resurfaced. "Agnes, would you know if Becca or Frank ever received treatment at Onward Home? The phone number is listed in Frank's cell phone contacts."

"Frank did, but only for a short time. It was too expensive. They tried everything to keep him there. They offered to pay half of his online courses so he could get a computer technician diploma. They even promised him a job after he completed the program. Can you imagine?"

"What happened?"

"Like I said, Frank couldn't afford it. He didn't want me to help him pay for it either." She frowned in annoyance. "Something else bothered him about the program. He told me it sounded suspicious, and that he would have turned it down even if he had the money to pay for it."

Michael asked, "What did he find suspicious about it?"

Agnes smiled. "He said there was no such thing as a free lunch in life."

High-pitched squeals of laughter sounded in the staircase. Cory and his sister Olivia ran into the living room, giggling and waving large sheets of paper.

Agnes welcomed them into her arms, then said in a quiet voice, "Now children, remember, you mustn't run in the house. What have you got there?"

The children held up their drawings for Agnes to see. Splashes of deep reds, blues, and yellows displayed their energy and creativity.

"Oh, these drawings are beautiful." Agnes smiled at them. "You're both wonderful artists."

"They're for you, Granny," Cory said.

"For you," Olivia echoed.

"Well, thank you very much," Agnes said.

As she held the drawings up to admire them, I noticed scribbling on the reverse side. Some sort of repetitive pattern.

"I tell you what," Agnes said to the children. "While I chat with my visitors, why don't you go back upstairs and draw more beautiful paintings for me?"

"Like what?" Cory asked.

"Surprise me."

The children ran off, giggling all the way up the stairs.

I held out my hand. "Agnes, may I see the drawings?"

"Of course." Her face brimmed with pride as she passed them to me.

I didn't want to take away from her moment, so I made an effort to admire them. "They're so colorful and pretty." I smiled at her, then flipped the papers over. "Hmm... Someone's been practicing their signature."

Michael studied them. "Lotty Banks. Do you know anyone by that name, Agnes?"

"Can't say that I do," she said.

I handed her the papers. "What about the handwriting? Do you recognize it?"

She squinted at the signatures. "No, I definitely don't."

"Are these papers from a store-bought supply?"

"No. Becca occasionally brought home a stack of paper from work. The kids use them for their drawings."

Michael leaned forward. "Do you have any more paper?"

"Yes," Agnes said. "A couple of letter-sized boxes."

"May we see them?" he asked.

"Why? Do you think the writing is connected to Becca?"

"Maybe."

"I'll go get them." She hurried upstairs.

"What do you think, Michael?" I whispered.

"Let me check something." He accessed the photos on his phone. "Here's a photo of Becca's driver's license that I took in her hotel room. I'm no writing analyst, but the capital *L* in Lotty looks a lot like the *L* in Becca Landry's signature." He zoomed in on it and showed it to me.

I held the sheet with the Lotty Banks signature next to it. "You're right. It's similar, but the slant of the writing is different. Do you think Becca was planning on changing her identity?"

"It's possible. We'll have to compare other letters in both names to be sure."

Footsteps sounded on the staircase.

Michael tucked his phone away.

"Here you go." Agnes deposited the boxes on the coffee table.

Michael and I took a box each. We flipped through the papers and withdrew the ones with handwriting on them. We ended up with twenty sheets between us.

I was about to put the rest of the papers back into the boxes when I noticed something I'd missed earlier. "Agnes, there are two keys taped to the bottom of this box."

"Oh, they must be the extra keys to the front door of the office building and the company office where Becca works. She sometimes misplaced her keys and had ordered duplicates in case."

"She had keys to the building and to the office?"

"Yes, she often worked late hours. Her boss gave her a set of keys so she could lock up on her own."

Michael held the twenty sheets of paper we'd retrieved. "Agnes, we'd like to keep this pile, if it's okay with you."

"Be my guest," she said. "The kids have more than enough paper left for their drawings. Can you wait a moment? I'll be right back." She headed for the stairs.

A nod from Michael triggered my next move. I reached for the keys, tore them out of the box, then dropped them into my handbag. I placed the leftover piles of papers back into the boxes.

Agnes returned with a large envelope. "Here you go. You can put your sheets in here. What do you make of the rows of signatures on them?"

Michael slid the thin pile of sheets into the envelope. "We're not sure at this point, but we'll check it out." He stood up.

I grabbed my handbag. "Agnes, please call us if you hear from Frank."

Worry strained her features. She said in a soft voice, "It's been so long. I'm afraid I'll never hear from him again."

As we drove away, Michael smiled. "You did it. You swiped the keys."

"And I feel horrible about it."

23

———

As soon as Michael and I stepped into the lobby, Eric waved us over to the front desk.

"The cops just left." He pulled out a newspaper from under the counter and placed it before us. "Did you know you guys made the front page headlines?"

I gaped at a photo of Michael and me leaning over Dylan. My guess was that a bystander had taken the shot and sold it to the newspaper.

"This is the first we've seen of it," Michael said.

"You can keep the newspaper if you want," Eric said. "The article says you tried to save Dylan's life."

"So did the paramedics."

Eric grimaced. "What a downer. The staff is walking around in a daze. We just can't wrap our heads around what happened to Dylan. What the hell was he doing there?"

"You mentioned the cops were here." Michael folded the newspaper and tucked it under his arm.

"They questioned me, but I didn't know anything. I never hung out with Dylan after work. They interviewed the entire staff this morning."

Michael's phone rang. He glanced at the display but didn't answer. "Thanks for the paper, Eric. Gotta run." He took my hand and we hurried toward the elevators.

"What's the rush, Michael?"

His face lit up. "My tech friend just called. He sent me the video. Let's hope it contains the missing pieces to the puzzle."

~

His wish was granted minutes later.

Michael's tech friend had sent the video, along with an explanation for the delay. He'd had a bicycle accident and suffered a slight concussion. Doctors recommended that he remain in the hospital under observation for a few days to make sure no complications developed.

Michael and I settled on the sofa and watched the video on his laptop. The footage ran from five-thirty Friday afternoon to eight o'clock that evening. I didn't take my eyes off the screen as it played out.

The images were somewhat blurry in parts, but it was easy to recognize the people we knew, like Eric and Andy. The lineup of guests checking in or out at the front desk was in constant flux, as was the number of people crossing the lobby.

The timestamp on the video showed five-forty the afternoon Becca arrived. After she registered at the front desk, she walked toward the elevators and disappeared into a crowd of people wearing business suits or sports attire.

"There are too many people in the lobby," I said. "We can't see if Becca got into the elevator or not."

"We have to assume she did," Michael said.

The subsequent portion of the video dragged on for about twenty minutes until Frank arrived at six. He sat on a chair in the lobby for about ten minutes, after which he took out his phone and made a call.

"That's when he was trying to call Becca," I said.

After several more futile attempts on his phone, Frank stood up and walked over to the front desk. He circumvented waiting customers and approached Andy to speak with him.

What looked like a heated argument followed, with Frank waving his hands in the air and pointing a finger at Andy.

Andy left the customer he was serving and moved further along the counter to access another computer. He appeared to be scanning hotel records. He shook his head at Frank, who became visibly upset.

"I bet that's when Andy noticed Becca's name wasn't in the registry, but he couldn't tell Frank," Michael said. "Client privacy."

"The timestamp shows it's six-thirty," I said. "Frank should be heading for the elevators at any moment."

After exchanging more heated words with Andy, Frank stormed from the front desk and made a beeline toward the elevators.

"Dylan told us Frank arrived at the lounge and stayed there about half an hour. That would take us to seven o'clock."

The screen suddenly went black.

"Is that it?" I asked.

"Let's wait it out," Michael said. "There has to be more."

Sure enough, his tech friend appended video clips of passengers inside the hotel elevators. Similar to the previous segment we'd viewed, the clips spanned between five and eight o'clock in the evening.

Dylan appeared in a handful of clips, his food cart taking up much of the space in one of the elevator cars before he got off at the sixth floor. It felt surreal. Seeing him almost negated the fact he was dead.

In another clip, Frank and several passengers took another elevator from the ground floor at six thirty-five. Frank was alone as he stepped out into the lounge.

Another clip showed Frank leaving the lounge and riding the elevator down with three other passengers. The car jolted and the passengers looked worried. Frank was standing by the elevator panel. He pushed a button to open the doors, and everyone exited the elevator.

"What the hell—" Michael replayed the last segment of the video and paused it just before the elevator jolted.

"There was a problem with the elevator." I verified the time-stamp. "It happened at seven o'clock. What floor did the elevator stop on?"

He leaned in. "It's hard to tell. The image is fuzzy."

"Maybe the sixth floor? Becca's floor?"

"Let's not jump to conclusions, Megan."

The video went black for a long second. It reopened with a scene of the underground parking lot. We watched for ten minutes as a succession of vehicles drove out.

"Can you speed it up, Michael? Nothing's happening."

"No. I don't want to miss anything."

Half an hour later, my eyes were burning from staring at the screen. An assortment of cars, vans, and motorbikes had driven out of the parking. No sign of Frank or anyone else we knew.

I was about to call it quits when Michael pointed to the screen. "That must be Frank's red truck. You can see him clearly through the driver's window."

"The timestamp indicates seven-thirty," I said. "It took him a long time to get to the parking area. Even if we assume it was six or seven flights of stairs down from where he got off the elevator."

"Let's watch the rest of it. Then we'll go see Eric and ask if he knows anything about the elevator glitch."

"What about the regular occupant of room 634? Did your tech friend send you that information?"

Michael paused the video. "I'll check my email." Moments later, he said, "No email. He probably forgot. I'll send him a reminder."

We watched the rest of the video. It only lasted another minute, and we didn't notice anything extraordinary.

The screen went black for the final time.

We caught up with Eric as he was leaving the main floor coffee shop, a food tray in his hand.

"Yeah, I remember someone complaining about an elevator malfunction," he said in reply to Michael's question. "I think it was Friday. I can't be sure."

"Do you know what floor it stopped on?"

"No. You got me there. The maintenance superintendent would probably know."

"Can you find out?"

Eric hesitated. "I'm on my dinner break. How about I let you know in about an hour?"

"Sounds good."

Michael and I ordered takeout from the coffee shop before we returned to our suite. At least the trip downstairs wasn't a complete waste.

True to his word, Eric contacted Michael by early evening. The superintendent confirmed the elevator malfunction had occurred last Friday evening. The cause was electrical. The elevator car had stopped on the sixth floor and had remained inoperable for about fifteen minutes.

I sat next to Michael on the sofa and tested my theory. "It's quite a coincidence that the elevator stopped on the sixth floor, don't you think?"

"Elevator glitches are known to happen," he said.

"I know, but what if it wasn't a glitch?"

"What are you getting at?"

"You saw the video. Frank was standing by the panel in the elevator."

"You think Frank tampered with the buttons?"

"I admit it's only a theory. I realize we would need proof."

"Good, because the next step will take us to the parking area. We're going to interview whoever is in charge there."

~

True to his name, Max looked more like a limousine chauffeur than a parking lot supervisor. A limo driver hat over a dark service uniform struck me as a peculiar dress code for the job until I asked him about it.

"Management needs chauffeur service for VIPs a few times a week," Max said. "It means big tips if I'm ready to go. So here I am." He chuckled, then adjusted his hat over a head of thick white hair. "What can I do for you folks?"

Michael asked, "Were you working last Friday evening?"

"Why do you want to know?" Max hesitated. "Are you with the police?"

"No, we're not cops."

"All the better. I've had my share of them this week. You probably heard about the dead woman they found in a hotel room here. It was all over the news."

"Yes, we did."

"The police interrogated my staff at all hours, disturbed our schedules, and caused me to miss a limo opportunity." Max grunted. "To answer your question, I worked till nine Friday evening. I was on patrol duty."

"Patrol duty?"

"It's an inside term we use. It means I make the rounds, make sure everything is copacetic."

Michael asked, "Did you happen to see a man with a slight limp, short military-style haircut, at about seven-thirty that evening? He drives a red pickup."

"Yes," Max said. "I remember a fella like that. He sat in his pickup truck for the longest time. He was trying to reach someone on his phone, over and over. I went closer and noticed he was crying. He spotted me and drove out of the parking like a bat from hell."

"Did the police question you about him?" I asked Max.

"Yes, and I told them the same story." A frown accentuated the lines in his forehead. "Funny thing. They asked me about some other fella too."

"Connected to an investigation?" Michael asked.

Max shrugged. "I wouldn't know."

"Did they mention a name?"

"No."

"How about a description of the man or his vehicle?"

Max hesitated. "You know, you sure ask a lot of questions."

"We're private investigators looking for a missing person," Michael said, twisting the truth again.

"Well, you should have said so from the start." He laughed. "He was middle-aged and wore a red baseball cap. So did a hundred other fellas in the hotel. We had a baseball game in town that night." He let out a hearty laugh.

We held back from discussing what we'd learned from Max until the elevator doors opened to our penthouse suite.

Michael voiced his thoughts. "Who the hell is that mystery man in the red baseball cap the police were asking Max about?"

"It could be a coincidence," I said, "but Evelyn mentioned how a man in a baseball cap had bumped into her outside her hotel room that Friday."

"Like Max said, lots of guys wore baseball caps that day."

"It could have been Jerry. He had a bunch of red baseball caps in his office."

"You're picking at straws."

"No, I'm not. Jerry is on our list of suspects."

"Which includes Dylan, Randall Thorne, and the regular occupant of room 634."

And Frank, I held back from saying.

"Too bad the police couldn't offer Max a definite description of the guy they were looking for or his car," Michael said.

"Maybe he didn't drive here," I said. "He could have taken a taxi or walked to the hotel."

"Could be." He reached for a bottle of water from the fridge and handed me one. "It's been a busy week, hasn't it?"

"Tell me about it. More surprises at every turn."

Worst of all, I still hadn't begun that ghostwriting project for my client. How could I? I'd spent practically every minute working with Michael. Of course, I didn't blame him. I'd agreed to help him. But my other plans were now completely derailed.

Michael took a sip of water. "An agent from the Anti-Fraud Center came knocking at Frank's door looking for him, but nobody knows why. Then Agnes handed us boxes containing papers that Becca brought home from the office. Dozens of sheets with rows of someone's signature on them."

"We still have to study them more closely, by the way."

"Right. And all those other lingering questions we need to resolve. What about the two thousand dollars in Becca's purse? Was it a cash payment from Jerry for her work or something else? What was she going to do with the money?"

I added my share. "What was she planning to do about her pregnancy?"

"We still don't know how she died."

"Or who killed her."

Michael sighed. "I think it's time to compare notes with Grist."

As much as I disliked the detective's attitude, I had to agree. "I think so too."

His phone rang and he answered. "Yes, it's me... I'm so sorry, Agnes... No trouble at all. See you soon." He blinked hard.

I braced myself for bad news. "What's wrong?"

Confusion and despair clouded his expression. "You won't believe this. The cops found Frank. He's dead."

24

———

Had I been right about Frank all along?

Had remorse overtaken him?

Or had someone killed him for the same reason they'd killed Becca?

Where did the police find Frank's body?

How long had he been dead?

These questions would remain unanswered until Michael and I arrived at Frank's home and spoke with Agnes.

Poor woman. First Becca, now her son.

I couldn't possibly imagine how sick with grief she must have felt when the police arrived at her doorstep with the horrible news. She'd told us just the other night how she feared she would never hear from Frank again.

Her instincts were right.

Mother's intuition.

Michael parked behind a police cruiser and an unmarked car. Although a lamppost cast a hazy glow over the quiet suburban street, I expected a less tranquil scene inside Frank's home.

A uniformed officer opened the front door for us.

Detective Grist sat speaking with Agnes in the living room. He paused to acknowledge us with a nod, which indicated he wasn't surprised to see us. "We'll keep you informed of any developments," he said to Agnes before addressing us. "Good of you to make it. Come sit down."

Agnes sat in the armchair, her face pale and lined with weariness. She clutched a wad of tissues in preparation for the next stream of tears.

Michael and I expressed our condolences to her, then took our places on the sofa opposite the detective.

"I wasn't going to share the latest findings with you," the detective said, "but Agnes asked me to. As she told you on the phone, we discovered Frank's body this evening."

At the mention of her son's name, Agnes stiffened.

A cool breeze blew through the open window, causing the sheer curtains to flutter. I wondered about the timing. It was as if Frank's spirit were saying, "Hey! I'm still here."

"Where did you find him?" Michael asked the detective.

"In his car, near the National Military Cemetery of the Canadian Forces."

"That cemetery is where his friend Nino was buried," Agnes said. "Frank often told me he wanted to be buried in the same —" She choked up, wiped away fresh tears.

I swallowed hard.

Michael asked the detective, "Do you suspect foul play?"

"We don't know yet. It's too early in the investigation."

Agnes cleared her throat. "Detective Grist, I'm not very good at this, but if I understood you earlier, you said my son might have killed himself."

"I've asked forensics to put a rush on the autopsy," he said to her. "We'll know more once the initial report comes in."

"And when is that?" Agnes asked.

"In the next day or so." He switched his attention to Michael and me. "Agnes tells me you were trying to locate Frank."

An open-ended remark. What was he getting at?

"Yes, but we weren't successful," Michael said.

The detective waited, but Michael offered no additional details. "Is there anything you can tell me about your last conversation with Frank that would explain what happened?"

"Not really."

Detective Grist abruptly stood up. "Let's take this outside. Excuse us, Agnes."

Michael and I left a bewildered Agnes staring after us as we followed the detective out the front door.

"Give us some privacy, constable," the detective said to the uniformed officer.

"Yes, sir." The constable walked over to his cruiser and lit a cigarette.

Detective Grist kept his eyes on us. "I hear you interviewed the staff at the Dorfin Hotel. When were you planning on sharing the details with me?"

"When we had enough evidence to clear Frank's name in Becca's murder," Michael said.

"What makes you think she was murdered?"

"The same reason you thought Frank was a prime suspect."

"He might still be. I don't know of any husband who wouldn't notify the police that his wife went missing."

"She wasn't missing," Michael said. "Frank had no contact with her for a few hours. It didn't merit a call."

I happened to look at the house. A figure stood behind the sheer curtains in the living room, right by the open window. Was Agnes listening to our conversation?

"In any case, Frank wasn't responsible for Becca's death," Michael said.

My pulse quickened. Was Michael going to divulge the information we'd gathered? Reveal his source?

Detective Grist raised an eyebrow. "You must have proof on hand to make a statement like that about Frank. It's time to share what you know."

"I can't. Journalistic privilege."

My heart pumped faster as the men stared each other down with heated determination. Would it come to blows?

"You weren't always this belligerent, Michael." The detective grinned, easing the tension.

"When it comes to protecting my sources, I am."

The detective briefly looked away. "I'll ask again. Have you and Megan unearthed any information that might help my investigation?"

I didn't answer. This was clearly Michael's battle. I wasn't about to interfere in their head-butting session.

"It depends," Michael said.

"On what?"

"On whether or not we can make a fair trade."

Detective Grist laughed. "In your dreams."

"Then I guess we have nothing more to talk about. Come on, Megan. We'll go say goodbye to Agnes."

"Okay, okay. I'm game for a fair trade." The detective raised his hands in the air. "Damn, you strike a hard bargain."

Michael waited.

"I watched the news report about your trip to the ByWard Market last night," the detective said. "You have time to stick your neck out into matters that landed you and Megan in the headlines, but you can't help with my investigation. Is that it?"

"We weren't trying to be heroes," Michael shot back. "We were trying to save Dylan, the employee at the Dorfin Hotel." He stopped. "They told me he didn't make it."

Detective Grist's tone softened. "Sorry about that. One of our homicide investigators believes it was a gang-related murder. He contacted the joint police task force. They investigate shootings that involve suspected gang members and alleged fentanyl trafficking."

"I assume surveillance video is available in the area."

"Yes. We have access to it."

Michael said nothing. Like me, he was probably thinking

that the street video of the shooting was a better alternative to the video he'd taken with his phone.

The detective asked, "Why were you and Megan tailing Dylan anyway?"

Michael crossed his arms. "Who said anything about tailing him?"

"We worked together on that drug surveillance project in Toronto for a month. I think we know each other's shadowing strategies damn well by now. Don't try to tell me you happened to be in the ByWard Market by fluke when Dylan got shot."

"You're right." Michael let his hands drop to his side. "We followed him because we believed he was implicated in Becca's murder."

"How?"

"He worked the delivery room service at the hotel Friday afternoon. We suspect he tampered with the wine he delivered to her room."

Detective Grist looked puzzled. "Tampered? How?"

"He could have dropped GHB into the decanter."

A glimmer of awareness shone in the detective's eyes. "Not quite there but damn close."

"What do you mean?"

"I'll let you in on something. GHB didn't kill Becca. We suspect it was fentanyl, but autopsy results aren't conclusive yet."

"Fentanyl?" I said to the detective. "Frank was adamant that Becca wasn't a user."

"Megan, if there's one thing I've learned in my line of work," the detective said, raising his chin, "it's that you can't trust anyone. People will lie to get themselves out of trouble."

Michael stepped in. "Before the paramedics arrived, Dylan told me he'd sold fentanyl to someone Friday afternoon. He passed out before I could get a name. Maybe they're the same pills you found in Becca's purse, maybe not. In any case, Frank told us they were for his usage."

Detective Grist's expression didn't reveal whether or not he knew about Dylan's involvement in the drug trade or Frank's addiction to fentanyl. "So you're saying Dylan was involved somehow?"

"I don't think he had a personal motive for murder. He might have been working for someone else."

The detective nodded. "Fair assumption."

I needed clarification on one particular point. "Detective, do you have proof that Becca took fentanyl?"

"Right now, I don't. Forensics are scratching their heads over that one too. The sleeve of fentanyl pills we confiscated from Becca's purse was sealed. The contents of her stomach revealed no ingestion of fentanyl pills—not even microscopic particles. They examined the possibility she'd used a fentanyl patch or nasal spray but found nothing, yet her body exhibited all the symptoms. It doesn't take much. Just two milligrams of pure fentanyl can be lethal." He pressed his lips together. "We've done our homework, but it hasn't made a dent in the case."

"What about intravenous fentanyl?" Michael asked him.

Doubt registered on Detective Grist's face. "Not likely. It's difficult to obtain. It's mainly used by medical professionals for anesthesia and analgesia."

"What about injection?" I asked. "If liquid fentanyl exists, that is."

"To my knowledge, it doesn't," the detective said, "though we never know what's going to hit the streets next."

"Ottawa is supposed to be one of the safest cities in the country," I said.

The detective gave me a discerning look. "Every city has a dark underbelly."

"I told you about the article I'm researching on fentanyl," Michael said to him. "I could use more information. How about repaying that favor you owe me from our time in Toronto?"

"Name it."

"A ride-along with Ottawa's drug bust unit."

Detective Grist chuckled and wagged a forefinger at him. "You're as sharp as ever, you know that? How much longer will you be in town?"

"A few days."

The detective rubbed his chin. "Well, I can't say if anything definite is in the works, but if something goes down soon, I'll let you know."

I nudged Michael.

He caught on. "Megan is part of my research team. I'd like her to come along."

"Out of the question," the detective said. "It's too risky."

Before I gave it a second thought, I heard myself blurting, "Detective, don't you trust me?"

"It's not about trust," he said. "It's about keeping you safe during a situation that could turn violent."

"Then that's your job, isn't it? If you can keep Michael safe, you can keep me safe too."

He shook his head at the sky, then said, "Okay. But only if you both promise to stay within designated limits."

"No problem," Michael said.

"Good. Let's go back inside."

We entered the living room to find Agnes holding a framed photo of Frank and Becca. She wiped her eyes with a tissue. "I don't care what you think, Detective. My son was heartbroken over Becca's death. There's no way he could have killed her."

As I suspected, she'd overheard our conversation.

Agnes sniffed. "I hope you realize that Frank's note wasn't an admission of guilt."

"What note?" Michael asked.

Detective Grist hastily interjected, "I'm not in a position to share that information right now."

Agnes pointed a finger at him. "If you don't tell them, I will."

The detective reluctantly agreed. To Michael and me, he said, "What I'm about to share with you is confidential. It stays within these walls, or I'll charge each of you with obstructing an investigation. Is that clear?"

"No problem," Michael said. "We've already established we're on the same side. Right, Megan?"

"Right."

"You can count on my discretion too," Agnes said, squaring her shoulders.

"We found a note in Frank's jacket," the detective said. "Agnes confirmed it's in his handwriting. The text read: 'Mom and kids, I'm sorry.' That's all he wrote."

"What do you make of it?" Michael asked him.

He raised his hands. "I won't go there. It's pure speculation at this point."

"Frank was depressed because he lost the love of his life." Agnes placed the framed photo back on the corner table. "Life let him down."

Silence intensified the awkward moment.

Detective Grist said, "Okay, I'm done here. Agnes, I'll keep in touch with you over the next few days." He gave us a nod, then let himself out.

A frown lingered across Michael's forehead as we drove back to the hotel. His eyes were on the road, but his mind was elsewhere.

"Care to share your thoughts?" I asked.

"We're spinning our wheels," he said.

"How?"

"We've only eliminated Frank as a suspect."

"If Dylan didn't kill Becca, we can eliminate him too."

"Not so fast. I'm having second thoughts about the guy's confession."

"Why?"

"Like I told the detective, Dylan could be protecting someone. We don't know the final results of Becca's autopsy yet either. It could throw us another curve."

"What about Jerry, Randall, and the regular occupant of room 634?"

"The first two suspects are still in the running, but we don't have enough evidence yet to build a case against either of them. The unknown room occupant is still haunting us." He let out a frustrated sigh.

"So you're saying our investigation is back to square one."

"If you put it that way, yes. We need a piece of evidence that can point us in the right direction." He tightened his grip on the steering wheel. "Damn! Where the hell did we go wrong?"

25

We spread out the papers we'd obtained from Agnes in rows of four by five on the hardwood floor in our suite. The same signature repeated itself multiple times on each sheet, whether it was Lotty Banks, Tina Beaulieu, Barbara Lord, or another name.

Michael and I compared the handwriting on every sheet and concluded that the same person had signed them: Becca Landry.

"The capital *B* and the capital *L* are similar to the way Becca signed her real name," I said. "The vowels are similar too. See these closed loops in the letter *a* in the names? It has to be her handwriting."

Michael stood back and examined the papers. "Question is, why was Becca practicing to write those signatures?"

"Tasha said Becca felt overwhelmed by the duties of her job —especially when it came to signing documents. Maybe it's work related."

"It can't pertain to legal or business papers. Jerry Leduc is the only authorized signature for the company."

"How do you know this?"

"He's listed on the Internet as the sole principal. Besides, if Becca were a partner, Frank or Agnes would have mentioned it."

An image of the boxes with affixed seals flashed through my mind. "Remember the documents under Jerry's desk? What if Jerry asked Becca to add her signature to his on the certificates? Two signatures would make them appear more official when they're handed out to successful candidates."

"Could be. Then why wouldn't she just sign her real name?" He gave it more thought. "Maybe we're on the wrong track."

"In what way?"

"Maybe Becca was planning to change her identity for one reason or another and skip town."

"Skip town? And leave behind her husband and family? She was pregnant, Michael."

He ran a hand through his hair. "This whole case is plain crazy. Let's put it aside for now and review the video again. I can't shake the feeling we missed something."

I picked up the papers and put them in a pile on the coffee table. Outside, dark clouds were sweeping across the sky, expanding their coverage over a lighter shade of gray. "Looks like a storm is coming our way."

"You can say that again." He took his usual spot on the sofa and flipped open his laptop. "We have until Sunday to crack open this investigation. Do you really have to get back to work on Monday?"

"Yes, I do."

"Can't you ask Bradford Publishing for extra time off?"

"No, I can't. I'm way behind schedule as it is. I haven't even started my ghostwriting project, and it's due in two weeks!"

"I'm in a crunch too," Michael said. "The newspaper has something else lined up for me next week."

I sat next to him. "We've spent all our time working on this case. We need to put something into perspective. It's Detective Grist's responsibility to investigate Becca's death—not ours."

"I'm well aware of that. But I promised Agnes and you promised Tasha that we'd get involved. Doesn't our word count for anything anymore?"

"Of course, it does."

He tapped the keyboard harder than usual. "I hate seeing murder go unpunished."

"We can only do so much. We don't wear police badges. We don't have access to the places they do."

A twinkle lit up Michael's eyes. "Has that ever stopped us?"

I sat upright. "Oh, no, you don't. What trouble are you concocting now?"

"It's time we visit Jerry's office again."

"That's not a good idea. He almost threw us out the last time we were there."

"Who said anything about going there during business hours?" He gave me an impish grin.

Uh-oh. I was afraid of that. "You can't break in. It's illegal. I know we've done it before—and it scared me to death every time—but one of these days we're going to get caught."

"You're forgetting something. We have Becca's keys to Jerry's office."

I grabbed my handbag and dug out the keys. "Here. I want nothing to do with them."

Michael took them. "You're not serious." He slid the keys in his back pocket.

"I most certainly am. It's still considered a break-in in my books. We don't work there."

"We have no choice. Jerry might have already prepared course certificates for his graduates. I'll bet Becca signed them ahead of time using a fake name. We need to find them."

"Even if she signed them, what difference would it make?"

"It's considered fraud. It could be the reason the anti-fraud guy went to Becca's home."

"How would criminal charges hold up? Becca's dead."

"Jerry's not."

Michael's phone rang. He answered. "Hi. Didn't think I'd hear back from you so soon... Okay. Sure. See you then." He hung up. "Change of plans. That was Grist. We have a ride-along on a drug bust tonight. He wants to brief us beforehand and asked that we meet him at the station in an hour."

Detective Grist introduced us to Detective Sergeant O'Rourke of the Ottawa Police Service—or OPS—Drug Unit. In a deep voice matched by a dark police uniform and a commanding stance at six-foot-four, Detective O'Rourke briefed us on the upcoming undercover operation. A raid of six residences and businesses across Ottawa would take place simultaneously tonight. We were scheduled to ride with Detective O'Rourke and his team to a suburban home in Kanata where illegal drugs were allegedly being produced.

Before we left the police station, Detective O'Rourke brought us up to date on their war on drugs. "Our main goal is to curb the distribution and sale of deadly drugs on city streets," he said, his smooth head gleaming under the overhead lights. "Preventing overdoses is a major concern—especially during the city's summer music festivals. It's when there's easy access to illegal drugs, like ecstasy and other opioids. The danger increases when drugs like cocaine are cut with fentanyl. The effects can be unpredictable."

"Research shows the majority of illicit fentanyl in Canada comes from China," Michael said.

"Correct," the detective said. "The raw material is ordered online and delivered by mail or courier all over North America, often hidden within appliances like microwaves. It's cut with fillers and put through a pill-press machine to produce tablets. Fentanyl produced in an underground lab is less pure than the pharmaceutical version. There again, the user never knows what to expect. Effects can be fatal."

"How successful are your drug raids?"

"The Canada Border Services Agency—or CBSA—made about eleven thousand illicit-drug seizures a few years ago. Half of them arrived through the postal system."

"Can the CBSA open international letters and parcels if they suspect they contain drugs?" I asked him.

"If a CBSA officer suspects the item contains prohibited, controlled, or regulated goods, the answer is yes."

"On a related topic," Michael said, "I learned the members of the Hells Angels obtained legal personal production licenses for medical marijuana."

Detective O'Rourke nodded. "It's alleged they illegally sell the product to illicit dispensaries across the country. Law enforcement attempts at shutting them down are useless."

"Why useless?"

"We don't have the manpower to verify the identities behind the licenses. Furthermore, the gangs have access to the best legal and accounting advice available. If we bring them in to the station, they're out the same day."

"One last question," Michael said. "A lot of unsuspecting young people have died from fentanyl overdose. What is law enforcement doing to help prevent drug-related deaths?"

"We're increasing our efforts to educate the public about the risks." The detective gestured toward the pile of folders on his desk. "This is one month's worth of drug cases. Twenty percent of them are teens living in their parents' suburban home. They hold parties there to hide their drug usage. We do our best to get the word out about the risks, but with the recent stats on fentanyl usage, we expect the number of cases will increase. It's not just in Canada. Fentanyl overdoses are trending toward epidemic levels in other countries too."

A uniformed officer poked his head in the doorway. "We're ready to go, sir."

"Thank you." The detective explained to Michael and me, "It takes members of the drug unit a little more time to get ready. They wear protective gear to handle all the substances they might come into contact with during a raid. As an extra precaution, they carry naloxone. You heard of it?"

"We know all about naloxone," Michael said.

"Good." He stood up. "Now follow me."

Michael and I sat inside an unmarked police van a block down from the drug unit's target destination—a two-story home in a middle-class suburb of Ottawa. The tension in the van was as palpable as the rare torrent of summer hail hitting its roof like an endless round of bullets.

Detective O'Rourke stood by and focused on the visuals transmitted onscreen while communicating with his tactical team through their radio headsets. He occasionally exchanged several words with them. Otherwise, he sat in silence and waited.

The hail stopped. Rain replaced it with a nerve-racking pitter-patter over the next hour that had me wishing I'd brought along a pair of earplugs.

But we were stuck here until the mission was over, our bulletproof vests adding more weight to our bodies as if to ensure we stayed grounded.

"We've been monitoring this home for months after we got a tip from an anonymous source," Detective O'Rourke said. "An unhappy client."

"Sounds familiar," Michael said. "My best informants were people who were dissatisfied with the way they were treated by drug gangs."

"There's no loyalty in that business." The detective put a hand to his headset and listened. He uttered a command, then looked at us. "It's going down now."

Goosebumps rose along my arms.

Michael waited, hands clutched.

Loud popping sounds in the distance.
Gunshots!
Engines revving.
Squealing tires.
More shooting!
Vehicles roaring by.
Gunshots blasting the van!
We all hit the floor!

26

A strong grasp on my arm helped me to my feet.

Michael peered at me. "Megan? Are you okay?"

I processed what had happened. The weight of the bullet-proof vest had anchored me to the floor of the police van after I'd taken cover from the gunshots. "I think so." I checked my arms and legs. No blood. "And you?"

"I'm okay. But the detective isn't."

I looked down. Detective O'Rourke lay on his back in a heap, motionless.

A lump formed in my throat. "Oh, no! Is he dead?"

Michael leaned over and took his pulse. "He's still alive but he's been shot." He swiftly pulled back the Velcro flaps of the detective's bulletproof vest dotted with gunshot holes.

The back doors of the van burst open with a thunderous boom.

I jumped, my heart racing.

Two tactical team members scrambled in. "Everyone okay?" one of the officers asked.

Michael said, "The detective's been shot."

Just then Detective O'Rourke stirred. He slowly pushed himself up from the floor and asked, "Anyone hurt?"

Michael answered no.

"And you, sir?" the same officer asked the detective.

The detective rubbed his neck. "I'm fine. I got the wind blown out of me, that's all." He examined the bullet holes in the side of the van near where he'd been sitting. He removed his vest and studied it, then bagged it. "Bullet holes. This is going to forensics. You have an update, officer?"

"The dealer's gone," the other officer said. "We're in pursuit of him and the shooter. We're going to take them both down. You can be sure of it, sir."

"Thank you." The detective dismissed the two officers, then adjusted his headset and listened attentively for a minute or so. "They just caught the dealer," he said to us. "It's over."

~

Friday morning found Michael and me catching the local news on TV. The anchor announced:

"In strategic raids across Ottawa last night, members of the OPS Drug Unit arrested twenty-four people connected to the drug trafficking of counterfeit pills. At an early morning press conference, police told reporters they had seized enough chemicals to produce almost a million counterfeit pills at the rate of twenty thousand pills an hour. The citywide drug bust yielded cocaine, fentanyl, ecstasy, oxycodone pills, and marijuana. Police confiscated fourteen firearms, pill presses, vehicles, a sawed-off shotgun and a handgun, computers, cell phones, bomb-making materials, and four hundred thousand dollars in cash. More than three hundred criminal charges were laid. Suspects include two terrorists believed to have been on police radar."

"Feels terrific when justice is served, doesn't it?" Michael smiled and turned off the TV.

"It sure does." I took a sip of coffee and leaned into the sofa. I was groggy from not having slept enough, thanks to recurring nightmares about the shooting. Michael, on the other hand, snored without reserve as soon as his head hit the pillow.

He reached for his laptop. "We have a few things to wrap up before we—"

There was a knock at the door.

"Who could that be?" Michael crossed the floor to find out.

"Hope I'm not interrupting anything." Detective O'Rourke's deep voice resonated on the other side of the room.

"Not at all," Michael said. "Come on in."

As both men approached, I stood up, "Good morning, Detective. Would you like a cup of coffee?"

"No, thanks. I won't be staying long enough to enjoy it. I just dropped by to give you the lowdown on last night's raids." He unbuttoned his jacket, revealing a trimmer frame in a shirt and tie than in the protective police gear he'd worn yesterday.

"Please, have a seat." Michael gestured toward an armchair, then joined me on the sofa. "We watched the news report about the raids across the city. It sounds like you were successful."

"Yes, we closed down operations and got a load of drugs off the street. We discovered something in the materials we seized last night that might be of interest to you."

"Oh?" Michael leaned forward, indicating he was as curious as I was.

"We sent a sample of the suspected GHB out for testing to the lab. The results confirmed it wasn't GHB. It was liquid fentanyl."

So it does exist, I thought, recalling my question about it to Detective Grist the other day.

"We'd heard radio chat about it from time to time," the detective said. "We'd never seen fentanyl in liquid form on the illicit market in Canada, so it was never a concern until now. It's a real game changer for us."

"No kidding," Michael said. "I didn't realize you could get lab results so fast."

"We use specialized labs with rapid and sensitive detection facilities. They turn around requests for analysis in no time."

I asked the detective, "How potent is liquid fentanyl?"

"It's considered to be more powerful than the powder form of the drug."

"Handling fentanyl powder must be a tricky maneuver for the police during a raid."

"Definitely," Detective O'Rourke said. "Officers might be exposed to inhalation of fentanyl powder that's accidentally dispersed. That's why they wear protective gear during drug raids. They never know what they'll find."

"About liquid fentanyl," Michael said. "Do the police have access to any stats on its usage?"

"No," the detective said. "This liquid form is too new. We don't know how many people are using it on the street. It's a constant battle to warn the public about new illegal drugs hitting the market."

"It's a long shot, but would this drug bust have a connection to traffickers in the ByWard Market?"

"I'm not at liberty to confirm one way or the other. However, experience indicates there's always one in the group who's willing to rat on his pals to save his own skin. Which brings me to the next purpose of my visit." His gaze encompassed Michael and me. "We believe a male suspect detained in one of our city raids has a connection to the man's shooting you witnessed in the ByWard Market."

Michael stared at him. "You think he's Dylan's shooter?"

"Yes, and we'd like you and Megan to identify him." The detective's tone was calm but firm.

My stomach churned. Me? Identify a murderer?

"No problem," Michael said.

Terror mounted inside me. "No!"

"There's no need to be concerned," the detective said to me. "You'll be in another room and not visible to the suspect."

Perceiving my distress, Michael said, "Detective, I assumed you had access to surveillance video on the street."

"We do, but it's filmed overhead. It doesn't give us a clear view of the suspect's face."

"I have something you might find useful." Michael retrieved his phone. "I took this video of Dylan and the shooter in the ByWard Market." He played the video for him.

"Send me a copy here." The detective pulled out a business card and handed it to him. "Our tech team can enhance the video if necessary."

"I'll send it to you on condition that I remain an anonymous source."

"Agreed."

Michael caught the look of desperation on my face. "Also, Megan and I won't have to identify the suspect shooter."

The detective hesitated for a moment. "Fine."

Michael tapped buttons on his phone. "Sent. Detective, the news stated that you picked up two terrorist suspects and bomb-making materials as well. Do you attribute that to a lucky break?"

"I wish," Detective O'Rourke joked. "No, they'd been on our radar for some time. Alleged terrorists often get involved in drug trafficking to raise funds for their cause. Unfortunately, we believe there are more groups of sleeper cells out there who are getting ready to take action."

"Lone wolves who commit violent acts on their own are hard to find too."

"That's true, but sometimes we collect surprising inside information from the most unlikely sources. I can understand why you might have more success in that area than we do. Informants are more likely to talk to you because you don't carry a badge."

"That's true to a certain extent. I like to believe it's because my sources trust me to protect them in return."

"Trust goes a long way." The detective stood up. "Thanks for your time. And for the video. I have to drive back to the station to finish up some paperwork. Enjoy the rest of your visit here. And stay safe."

Stay safe?

Considering the schemes Michael and I were plotting, that wouldn't be easy.

27

Detective O'Rourke's bombshell about liquid fentanyl was difficult to fathom, though it put any doubts about the existence of the killer drug to rest.

"Liquid fentanyl," I said to Michael. "Can it get any worse?"

"Think of all the people trying out this stuff without knowing what the effects are."

I quivered at the memory of young Jacob in the ByWard Market and how the drugs he'd ingested had almost killed him. "Scary."

"Let's review something that might not be as scary. The hotel surveillance video from last Friday." He flipped open his laptop and set it on the coffee table.

Leaden clouds lingered in the sky like the interminable task ahead of us. We had several hours of video to watch again, but more slowly this time. It was going to be a long afternoon.

I poured more coffee into our mugs and joined Michael on the sofa. I needed a new target—a missing piece of solid evidence in the video that would assemble the puzzle into a coherent shape.

"We zoomed in on Frank the last time we watched the

video," I said. "Who do we focus on this time? An elusive man in a red baseball cap?"

"Why not?" Michael said.

"I was joking." I crossed the floor to a writing table to get a pen and paper, then returned to my seat. "I'll jot down the time-stamps of key scenes in the different video segments. Maybe we can work them into some kind of time sequence. It could help us close in on the murderer."

He smiled at me. "That's a smart idea."

"I get them now and then, you know." I poked him in the arm. "Okay. Let's find this killer so we can celebrate our victory in town tonight."

"We've already made plans for tonight, remember? We're popping into Jerry's office."

"Oh." I'd hoped he'd forgotten about it.

He tapped the keyboard. "Okay. Here we go."

While we watched the different segments of the video, I took notes of specific scenes and marked the timestamp next to each one.

First segment—main lobby:

5:00–5:30 pm: A mishmash of guests coming and going through the lobby. Business suits, T-shirts and shorts, baseball caps, seniors, teens, babies, luggage, and strollers. Eric and Andy serving guests at the front desk.

5:40 pm: Becca arrives at the hotel. She's wearing sunglasses and toting an overnight bag. She checks in at the front desk.

5:45 pm: Becca walks toward the elevators.

6:00 pm: Frank enters the lobby and sits in an armchair. He tries numerous times to reach Becca by phone.

6:00–6:30 pm: Guests coming and going through the lobby. Less business suits. More young couples. People in T-shirts, shorts, and baseball caps of all colors. Mothers with baby strollers and a couple of people in wheelchairs.

6:30 pm: Frank goes to the front desk and has angry words with Andy. He walks away toward the elevators.

Second segment—elevators:

5:00–5:10 pm: Numerous clips of passengers riding up and down the elevators. Men and women in sports attire, business suits. Teens, toddlers, seniors.

5:10 pm: Wally, the senior we met on the day we arrived at the hotel, gets into the elevator on the sixth floor. It confirms he went down to the restaurant before his wife Evelyn to reserve their seats for the early buffet dinner. He rides the elevator down with four other guests—all seniors.

5:10 pm: Dylan and his room service cart take another elevator up from the lobby. Roger (sleazy Roger!) gets in next. Two women in shorts and a chunky man wearing a red baseball cap and sunglasses squeeze into the elevator.

Note: Something about the man in the red baseball cap...

5:12 pm: Roger and the man wearing red baseball cap get off on the sixth floor. Dylan also steps off on the sixth floor to begin room service deliveries.

5:13 pm: Two women in shorts get off on the eighth floor. Empty elevator begins its downward ride.

5:15 pm: Other elevator rides up from lobby with five passengers. Two men (one short, the other tall), two young women, two teens. More red baseball caps, sunhats, and shorts.

5:16 pm: Elevator stops on the fourth floor. All get off except one woman wearing a floppy hat.

5:17 pm: Woman with floppy hat gets off on sixth floor.

5:20 pm: Other elevator in the lobby picks up three giggly teens and a mother holding a baby. Stops on the third and fourth floors to let them off.

5:23 pm: A couple and their toddler, an older woman, and a young woman with a backpack get into this elevator on the ninth floor. Elevator begins descent.

5:24 pm: The man in a red baseball cap and sunglasses gets into the same elevator on the sixth floor. Elevator stops on the way down to pick up two more people.

5:26 pm: Elevator empties on the main floor.

Note: Same chunky man in red baseball cap and sunglasses seen earlier. He rode the elevator up and got off on the sixth floor minutes before. Suspicious.

5:30 pm: Evelyn and two other women take the elevator down from the sixth floor.

5:46 pm: Becca rides the elevator up from the lobby with an elderly couple. The couple gets off on the fifth floor. Becca gets off on the sixth floor.

5:49 pm: Roger (again!) gets into elevator on sixth floor that Becca just exited. He rides down with a young woman holding a toddler's hand. Roger says something to the woman. She nods but doesn't make eye contact with him. Roger keeps chatting, but the woman doesn't answer. She pulls her kid closer to her and rushes out when the doors open to the lobby on the main floor. Roger strolls out.

5:51 pm: Other elevator coming down from lounge. Cocktail hour crowd: men in business suits; women in heels. Stops on the eighth floor to let off a man and a woman, then continues down to the lobby.

5:55 pm: At the end of his shift, Dylan pushes the food cart into an elevator on the sixth floor. Elevator stops on the fourth floor and two young men in jeans get on. They all get off on the main floor.

6:00 pm: Dylan rides the elevator up to the lounge to begin his shift at the bar.

6:00–7:00 pm: Less people in the elevator cars. Clips are sporadic within this time period. More young people dressed in casual wear, going out to pubs, restaurants, and festivities.

7:00 pm: Frank rides the elevator down from the lounge. Elevator malfunction. Frank and the other passengers get off on the sixth floor.

. . .

Third segment—underground parking:

7:00–7:30 pm: Clips of people driving in and out of the hotel parking area.

7:30 pm: Frank exits the parking in his pickup truck.

The screen went black.

"That's all of it." Michael sat back in the sofa. "Did anything stand out for you?"

"A man wearing a red baseball cap," I said.

"Yeah. I saw lots of them."

"I know, but I noticed something weird about a particular man in two of the elevator clips. Can we run the video again and verify these timestamps?" I handed him my notes.

Michael keyed in the information.

"There he is." I pointed to the image on the screen. "It's the same man in the red baseball cap and sunglasses in both sequences. He got off the elevator on the sixth floor and got back on minutes later. Don't you find that suspicious?"

"It's possible he had a quick visit with a friend."

"Exactly. In room 634."

"Becca's room?" He sat up. "Maybe he's our killer."

"I can't put my finger on it, but there's something familiar about him."

Michael leaned forward and gaped at the clip he'd paused. "It's a little fuzzy. All I see is an overweight middle-aged man in shorts and a loose sport shirt. His sunglasses and baseball cap hide most of his face."

"Can you zoom in?"

He enlarged the image. "Not good. It's fuzzier now."

There had to be a better way. "Let's pay close attention to the clips from the lobby, before and after the man gets in and out of the elevators. Here are the time sequences."

Michael entered the details from my notepad. We strained our eyes to locate the same man in a red baseball cap.

In the first clip, the timestamp at 5:10 pm showed the man entering the lobby and strolling toward the elevators. He disappeared into the flow of guests.

As the timestamp rolled to 5:26 pm in another clip, it showed the same man crossing the lobby and hurrying out the front door, his wobbly gait more familiar than ever.

I jumped to my feet. "I know him! It's Jerry Leduc!"

28

The hotel video had revealed a startling surprise.

Jerry Leduc had visited the Dorfin Hotel hours before we'd discovered Becca's lifeless body.

Had he been instrumental in her death?

Or had he visited the hotel for a different reason altogether?

After I voiced my suspicions, Michael said, "Jerry's presence at the hotel puts him at the top of our suspect list. Problem is, we need to find proof that he's involved in Becca's death."

I gave him *the look*. "This is the same man who pressured you to stop your investigation because his organization couldn't afford the bad press. I refuse to believe it's a coincidence that he happened to be at the hotel the same day Becca died."

"I realize that, but again, we need concrete evidence."

I wasn't giving up. "You had considered Dylan a suspect or, at the least, that he could have been protecting the killer. What if Jerry bribed him to drug the wine he delivered to Becca's room?"

"It's feasible, but we have no tangible proof that either one of these guys is involved, let alone that they knew each other." He raised his hands in the air. "What possible motive would either one have for wanting Becca out of the way? It doesn't make sense. For all we know, Jerry could have dropped by her room just to ask if everything was okay."

Maybe he was right. It was kind of creepy, but maybe Becca was used to Jerry controlling her work life. His weekend gift was merely an extension of that control over her.

"About the two thousand dollars in Becca's purse," Michael said. "What if Jerry popped in to give Becca her salary in cash? Your friend Tasha said he did that sometimes."

"Becca got paid every two weeks. I did the math. The money in her purse exceeded the expected eight hundred dollars."

"It's possible that Jerry knew things were tight financially and gave her an advance."

"I doubt it. Tasha said he was cheap."

Yet the matter of the extra money lingered in my mind, and I parsed it again.

Was the two thousand dollars in Becca's purse a payment for services of another sort?

Were Frank's initial suspicions about Becca right? Desperate to make extra money to afford her husband's meds, had Becca agreed to be Jerry's paid mistress?

Yet something had fueled Becca's argument with Jerry last Friday and pushed her over the edge. She'd shouted, "I can't do it anymore" and stomped out of the office. Was she referring to her affair with Jerry?

No way. Tasha insisted that Becca was a loyal wife.

Then there was Becca's job to consider. According to Tasha, Becca was a hostage. The pressure she'd felt at work was so palpable that she'd often complain about it to Tasha.

If Becca was so unhappy at work, why didn't she quit and look for another job? For some obscure reason, it was a damned if you do, damned if you don't situation.

Topping it off was Becca's pregnancy. Whose baby was it?

My mind was drowning in theories. I couldn't think straight anymore.

I peeked at Michael. He was replaying the lobby scenes on his laptop and pausing it at intervals.

His persistence inspired me to review my notes again. I studied the timestamps and activities I'd written next to each entry. If there was one way to prove Jerry had come in contact with Becca at the hotel, it was through a common timeline. They had to have been on the sixth floor during the same period of time.

My notes indicated that Jerry stepped out of the elevator on the sixth floor at 5:12 pm. He got back in the elevator at 5:24 pm and left the hotel at 5:26 pm.

Becca arrived at the hotel minutes later at 5:40 pm.

Simple deduction: They couldn't possibly have met. I was ecstatic!

I jumped up and tapped Michael's arm. "Listen to this!" I told him about my findings. "Jerry left the hotel minutes before Becca walked into the lobby. That's proof he didn't visit her hotel room."

He smiled. "Good job."

"There's more. The time sequence suggests that Becca was standing by the door to room 634 when Roger walked by, just like he claimed. She probably wanted to make sure no one was in the room, so she knocked before she let herself in with the keycard."

"Right. I noticed something else. Can I see your list?" He found what he was looking for and set the video timestamp to 5:10 pm. "Check out the guy in the red baseball cap. I think it's Jerry."

I peered at the screen. "You're right. It's him!"

"So Jerry and Dylan were in the same elevator going up. They got off on the sixth floor at the same time too."

"They didn't talk to each other in the elevator, though."

"It doesn't mean anything. Something could have gone down between them off camera."

My mind digressed. "You remember how Evelyn mentioned

that a man in a baseball cap had bumped into her, that he was in a rush? It could have been Jerry. The timing fits."

"Makes sense."

A sigh of relief trickled through me. "Finally. We're getting somewhere."

Michael's phone rang and he answered. "Hello, Detective."

Detective Grist? What did he want? Don't detectives ever take a day off?

"Liquid fentanyl?" Michael said, surprised. "That sure changes things. Okay. No problem. Thanks." He ended the call. "Megan, you won't believe this. Becca's final autopsy results confirm that liquid fentanyl killed her. It was in the wine."

My breath caught in my throat. "How awful!"

"No kidding. After Dylan got shot, he denied he'd drugged Becca's wine but confessed he sold fentanyl to someone that Friday. We've assumed all along that the fentanyl was in pill form, but it could have been liquid."

"What else did the detective say?"

"He asked us to keep it under wraps. Their investigation is moving in a new direction."

"Maybe they reviewed the hotel surveillance video like we did and reached the same conclusions. Either Dylan or Jerry drugged the wine and killed Becca."

Michael joined his hands in an enthusiastic clap. "Okay, let's work on that theory. We know Dylan got off the elevator with his cart to make room service deliveries. What puzzles me is why Jerry would hang around for fifteen minutes if Dylan had the fentanyl. Did he want to make sure Dylan completed his part of the deal?"

Another stark realization hit me. "Unless Jerry did it."

"I'm open to any feasible possibility."

I had one more wish. "If only we knew who the buyer was."

"The cops probably identified the buyer by now, especially if he purchased the drug on the street. Grist must have viewed the surveillance video of the transaction."

"So if Dylan or Jerry made the purchase last Friday—"

"Grist has his potential suspect." Michael closed his laptop. "We'll find out more when we visit Jerry's office later tonight."

"We're still going?"

"Why not?"

"It sounds as if Detective Grist is ready to wrap up the case."

"We can't assume anything. It's our last chance to dig up dirt on Jerry when he's not around."

"Okay. In the meantime, let's get ready for that fundraising event Tasha is holding this evening. Since it's going to benefit Jerry's organization, he'll probably be there."

Michael grinned. "I'm counting on it."

29

Jerry's latest fundraising event was housed in the Great Hall of the National Gallery of Canada, a contemporary light-filled structure of glass and granite.

I entertained the idea of ditching the event to tour the exceptional collection of sixty-five thousand works of art on display in the gallery, but I settled for an expansive view of Parliament Hill and the luscious green grounds instead.

A waiter whose tray balanced precariously from the weight of a dozen champagne glasses offered Michael and me a glass.

"Cheers." Michael clinked his glass with mine.

I whispered, "Let's hope we have something to cheer about later."

He scanned the room. "There must be close to two hundred people here. I saw Jerry when we walked in, but he was busy talking to other guests."

"I doubt he'll want to come over to talk to us."

"Look. Randall Thorne and Ed Finch are over there, next to the table of fancy appetizers." He gestured with his chin.

"Nothing like a couple of administrators getting together."

Michael beamed at me. "You're in a cheerful mood tonight."

Tasha sauntered toward us, a broad smile on her face. "Hi, Megan. So glad you could make it." She hugged me, then introduced herself to Michael. "Megan's told me so much about you, I feel as if I know you already." She laughed.

"Is that right?" Michael stared at me.

Tasha laughed. "Oh, you needn't worry. It's all good." She leaned in closer. "Michael, thanks for looking into you-know-what for me. I truly appreciate it. Without going into detail, are you any closer to finding out what happened?" She searched our faces.

"We'll know more in a few days," he said.

"I trust you to follow through on your promise," Tasha said, "but the lead detective in the case contacted me, and I met with him. Grist is his name. I have to say I wasn't too impressed."

"Why not?" I asked her.

She kept her voice low. "I told him about the pressure Becca had felt at work, her argument with the boss—everything I told you, Megan. He interpreted it as office gossip." She rolled her eyes.

"I've worked with the detective before," Michael said. "He usually takes every witness statement seriously."

"I hope so." She sighed. "Do you have any plans for later?"

My guard was up. "Uh...we might."

"If not, you should try to catch the Long Ma performance."

"Long Ma?"

"It's a giant, mechanical structure that's half-dragon and half-horse. It's named after a Chinese mythological creature. It weighs forty-five tons and stands at almost forty feet high. It'll be roaming the streets of Ottawa tonight during an urban theater performance. Long Ma and a huge mechanical spider named Kumo are supposed to meet in a battle. Pretty cool, eh?"

I was thrilled. It would make an excellent addition to my client's project. "It sounds like a once in a lifetime event."

Tasha went on. "Tens of thousands of people are expected to gather in the ByWard Market to see the creatures plod by. Many streets are closed till late tonight, so it's best if you go there on foot."

"We left the car in a parking lot in town and walked here, so we're good." I turned to Michael. "We can't afford to miss it."

"It would be a shame if you did," Tasha said.

Michael smiled. "Sounds like fun. I think we'll make a night of it then."

Tasha asked, "Have you been to the Sparks Street Mall or the Rideau Center? They have fantastic sales this time of the year."

"Not yet," I said. "We've been a little busy."

"Silly me." Tasha did a facepalm. "Of course, you've been busy." She smiled. "Well, it's time to mingle. Enjoy yourselves. I'll catch you later." She strolled off and greeted a party of four.

"That's what we should do," Michael said to me.

"What? Shop?" I was all for it.

"No, mingle."

No sooner had the words left Michael's mouth than another familiar face popped up.

Jerry held a glass of champagne in one hand and a shrimp appetizer in another. "Hello, Megan, Michael. I'm not at all surprised to see you at an event like this."

My pulse picked up speed. Here we were, within inches of a man whom we considered a potential murder suspect.

Michael stayed as cool as ever. "We thought we'd do our part to contribute to a worthy cause. Like you, Jerry, fighting drug addiction is a pet project of ours."

"Of course it is. I see we have mutual friends too." He tilted his head in Tasha's direction.

I forced a smile. "We've known each other for years."

"It certainly is a small world, isn't it?" Jerry swallowed the appetizer, then took a gulp of champagne. "How much longer will you be in Ottawa?"

Coming from him, the question was so intrusive.

"We're not sure," Michael said. "We're digging up so much new information that we might have to change our plans and stick around longer than expected."

"Are you still talking about your newspaper article on drug addiction?"

"And some."

Jerry's eyes narrowed. "Your persistent snooping into Becca's death won't win you any points with influential people who make things happen in this town."

Michael didn't break eye contact with him. "I don't play politics. I'm doing my duty as an investigative reporter."

"It's too bad you refuse to take my advice." Jerry's expression hardened.

Michael didn't flinch. "I'm tired of your threats, Jerry. Take them somewhere else."

Jerry drank more champagne and looked nervously around the room. Without another word, he made a beeline for an older woman wearing a sleeveless black dress and a string of pearls.

"What a pig-headed creep!" I said to Michael. "He's still trying to bulldoze you."

His jaw tightened. "If we ever dig up incriminating stuff on him, he'd better have friends in very high places."

A waiter came by with a tray of appetizers and napkins. Michael and I set our glasses on a table nearby, then chose two appetizers each and placed them on our napkins.

As we ate, I surveyed the people in the hall. No one else was familiar to me, though Jerry seemed to know everyone. He rapidly moved from one person to the next in his quest for donations, no doubt trying to talk up as many patrons as he could during the two-hour event.

I said to Michael, "How are we supposed to mingle when we don't know anyone here?"

"At least they have delicious food." He plucked two more

appetizers from a serving tray making the rounds and placed them on his napkin. He made them disappear moments before his phone alerted him to a message. He pulled it out and read the text. "It's from my tech friend. He knows the name of the regular occupant in room 634."

"Who is it?"

Michael leaned over and whispered, "Randall Thorne!"

My pulse quickened as I connected the dots. "You know what this means? He gave his keycard to Jerry for the weekend."

"And Jerry passed it along to Becca."

"I'm wondering if Becca knew she was entering Randall's hotel room. It would explain why she had his business card in her purse."

"Could be. I'd sure like to talk to Randall about it."

But the bureaucrat was nowhere in sight. "If you can find him, maybe you'll get your chance."

"In the meantime, let's circulate."

We meandered around clusters of people, searching for Randall. We'd almost reached the opposite side of the hall when a familiar figure broke out of a group standing a few feet away.

Randall himself.

He saw us and stopped, as if he were trying to retrieve our names from memory. He smiled. "Michael and Megan, we meet again." He shook hands with us. "Still visiting, are we?"

"Enjoying the evening," I said, leaving Michael to broach the more serious part of our conversation.

"Randall, I'd like to discuss something with you." Michael edged closer to him.

Randall misinterpreted his interest. "About our work at the foundation?"

"No. About how Becca Landry ended up dead in your hotel room."

Randall's forehead puckered in annoyance. Whether he was irritated by the question or by the fact we'd discovered his secret was hard to determine. "I travel across the country and stay at many hotels."

"We're talking about your room 634 at the Dorfin Hotel," Michael said. "And the keycard you gifted."

I admired Michael's strategy. It was a test to see if Randall would disclose that he'd gifted his keycard to Jerry, therefore betraying him.

But Randall's face remained deadpan. "I can only assume the woman was the recipient of a keycard I gifted to a business associate."

Michael waited. Silence remained his foolproof method of extracting more information.

Randall filled the gap in our conversation. "I sometimes gift a hotel keycard to an acquaintance or business associate when I'm away. It's basically a goodwill gesture. I hand them out but seldom, if ever, know who uses them."

Had I heard him right? "You're comfortable with gifting a keycard to your own hotel room to strangers?"

"Of course!" Randall huffed. "The room is already paid for. I simply ask for a replacement keycard and hand it out. It might as well be put to good use while I'm away."

I envisioned a variety of uses for his hotel room—some not so ethical, but I held back from verbalizing them. Who he chose to entrust the room to was solely his responsibility.

Michael took the premise a step further. "Do you have any idea who passed along your keycard last weekend?"

"No, and I wouldn't want to venture a guess for the sake of it. Above all, I wouldn't want to impede the police investigation by sharing unconfirmed information. Surely as a reporter, you can understand the implications of doing so."

A woman touched Randall's arm and asked if she could have a word with him.

"Excuse me." He joined her and they hastily moved away.

I whispered to Michael, "What do you make of Randall's keycard re-gifting?"

"It happens often. Randall knows and trusts the people he gifted his keycard to, so I suppose it's a matter of trust that the re-gifter will have the same mindset."

"Blind trust, if you ask me. Deliberate or not, that keycard was a factor in Becca's murder."

30

After we said our goodbyes to Tasha, we left the National Gallery and caught a glimpse of the towering 19th-century Notre-Dame Cathedral Basilica on Sussex Drive. A National Historic Site of Canada, its two prominent spires pierced a darkening sky streaked with ribbons of orange and pink.

Blocks ahead, dense crowds lined the streets in the ByWard Market, anticipating the arrival of Long Ma, the horse-dragon, and Kumo, the spider. The two gigantic mechanical creatures created a buzz in the crowd, a welcome distraction from our troubled thoughts about Becca's last hours. Like thousands of other spectators, we had our phones at the ready to capture the occasion.

It didn't disappoint.

Long Ma roared her way through densely populated streets, her head rearing, red eyes ablaze, smoke spewing from her nostrils. I watched in awe as the sixty-foot-long clanking creature rattled past us, spraying vapor and water on unsuspecting crowds. Long Ma captivated my imagination, rendering almost invisible the crew of more than a dozen people who operated it.

A stream of curious spectators followed Long Ma through

the city streets as she advanced to meet Kumo at the end of her journey. The battle between the two creatures promised to be epic, but Michael and I had to cut short our visit as the clock struck nine.

We had a battle of our own to wage.

~

The darkness of night provided the perfect cover for our secret operation.

Blocks from the ByWardMarket, we arrived at the four-story brick building that housed Jerry's office. Since it was located far from the crowds, we were confident we'd have access without being noticed.

We entered the building and locked the front door behind us, then climbed the stairs to the third floor. As we stepped into the hallway, we encountered the janitor pushing a cleaning cart at the other end.

He looked over his shoulder at us. "Good evening. Working late?"

Michael smiled. "Yeah."

We casually moved toward Jerry's office.

I whispered to Michael, "What if the janitor suspects we're intruders?"

"He won't. We have the keys to the place."

Michael took his time to retrieve the keys from his pocket. Once the janitor had entered another office, we slipped our hands into plastic gloves so as not to leave fingerprints on the door handle or any other surface.

Michael unlocked the door and we stepped inside. In case Jerry would inadvertently drive by the building and glance up at his office windows, we didn't turn on the overhead lights but used our flashlights to see our way around instead.

We hurried past the open offices sectioned off by glass partitions.

Becca's private office was up next. I was surprised to see the door ajar. At least the police tape had been removed, which meant this part of their investigation was complete.

We moved down the hallway to the first destination on our agenda: Jerry's office.

Michael slowly opened the door.

Stacks of documents littered every flat surface of the room, including the floor. Jerry had amassed more paper since the last time we were here.

"Business must be good," I said. "Where do we start?"

"Go through Jerry's desk," Michael said. "I'll check out the promo material on the table by the wall."

I peeked under the desk to find the same two boxes of certificates I'd noticed before, the red or gold seal affixed to the sheet on the cover. I removed the first page from each box.

What had been hidden from view earlier was the fact that the certificates were already signed by two people: a person whose signature was illegible and a woman whose name I recognized.

"Michael, come and see this." I shone my flashlight on one of the documents. "One of the signatures on this certificate is Lotty Banks. It's one of the pseudonyms on the sheets we collected from Agnes."

"And the other?"

"This one is signed by Tina Beaulieu. Another signature on the sheets she gave us. I'm guessing Becca signed them."

"Why she wouldn't sign her real name is what we need to find out. Let's keep looking for clues."

I thought about taking photos of the documents to show Detective Grist, but it would be hard to explain our presence in Jerry's office without incriminating ourselves.

I scanned the top of Jerry's desk. I was careful not to disrupt the order—or disorder—of the piles of paper. I gingerly sifted through them, lifting invoices, handwritten notes, and booklets here and there.

A shuffling noise behind me.

Papers cascaded to the floor at Michael's feet.

"It's okay. I got it." He bent down to retrieve them. Moments later, he chuckled. "Would you get a load of this?" He showed me a photo of Jerry with Randall Thorne and Ed Finch dressed in hunting pants and vests, standing in front of a building with the initials RA on it.

I studied it. "Is Randall Thorne carrying a rifle case?"

"Sure looks like it."

I pulled out my phone and did a quick search online. "The RA Gun Club is an indoor range in Ottawa that offers a venue for recreational and competitive shooting sports."

"Talk about the wild side of bureaucrats." He grinned.

"Where did you find the photo?"

"It was stuck in the baseboard behind the table. I didn't realize these guys were such good buddies."

"They know one another from work. It could have been a first-time, get-to-know-you meeting. What are you going to do with the photo?"

"Nothing." He put it back where he'd found it.

Ten minutes later, I hadn't discovered anything that even hinted at shady dealings—other than blank certificates with Becca's fake signatures on them. Not exactly the solid evidence that could incriminate a potential murderer.

I aimed the flashlight around the office. Michael was still rummaging through items on the floor beneath the table.

"I'm going to take a look around," I said.

He warned me, "I wouldn't go into any of the other offices if I were you."

"What about Becca's office? It's the second destination on our list."

He straightened up. "I'm done here. I'll go with you."

Becca's private mementos had been cleared from her desk. Even her framed certificates had vanished from the walls. If was as if she'd never existed. The police had probably packed them up and delivered them to Agnes.

Only a handful of books remained on a shelf in a narrow bookcase—dictionaries and how-to books on letter writing. Tools for the next employee.

Michael walked over to the desk and pulled open the top drawer. "There's nothing in here." He tried the side drawers. "Nothing much in here either. The cops must have seized whatever papers they considered important to their investigation."

"Maybe they found Becca's aliases like we did."

"Even so, we have no proof that they're linked to her death." Frustration filtered through his voice. "There's nothing more to see here. Let's go."

We were about to step into the corridor when a loud click broke the silence.

Someone had unlocked the outer door to the office!

31

---

ichael touched my arm and whispered, "Turn off your flashlight."

I did.

We carefully stepped back into Becca's office.

I closed the door halfway, leaving enough space for us to hide behind it.

Overhead lights suddenly lit up the corridor.

A set of heavy footsteps approached.

I caught a glimpse of Jerry Leduc as he strolled by.

"Okay, I'm here," he said.

My heart skipped a beat until I realized he was speaking to someone on his phone.

Jerry entered his office. "Listen to me, will you? You have nothing to worry about. That nosey detective is just fishing for information. He's got nothing on us."

A shuffling of papers.

"Yes, I realize you have a reputation to protect. We all do."

More things being moved around.

"Keep one thing in mind. The dead can't talk."

Something dropped to the floor with a loud thud.

A groan from Jerry. "No, no. A book fell, that's all."

A pause while the other party spoke.

Jerry raised his voice. "Will you give it a break? I told you there's no way he can trace the payoffs back to us. Now where did I put that flash drive, dammit?"

Behind me, Michael inhaled a quick breath.

Oh, no! Did he have the flash drive?

Jerry went on. "I remember hiding it under my promo stuff. Maybe it fell behind the table when I..." His voice strained as he bent over. "Nope. Not there."

More talking at the other end of the line.

"I keep telling you. There's no way that anti-fraud agent can trace the paperwork back to us."

More chatter by the other party.

"What do you mean, my bookkeeping is shoddy?" Anger ran through Jerry's voice. "If you hadn't been in such a hurry to capitalize on the project in the first place—"

The other party cut him off.

Jerry shouted, "What's that supposed to mean? I did my part, didn't I? And by the way, I don't take threats lightly."

A longer pause.

"That was your decision. I could have worked something out with her."

With *her*? Was he talking about Becca?

A short pause.

"No, it wasn't too late. Hello? Hello?"

He'd been cut off for good.

Anger erupted in a string of profanity from Jerry's mouth. Mumbling, he continued to search for the elusive flash drive.

The minutes dragged on.

Sweat gathered along my brow.

Behind me, Michael shifted from one foot to the other.

Jerry finally turned off the light in his office and moved down the corridor. He suddenly stopped and lingered in front of Becca's office.

Was he thinking about extending his search here—where Michael and I were hiding?

I held my breath. *No! No! Don't come in here!*

Grumbling to himself, Jerry advanced to the lobby. He turned off the overhead lights and left, locking the door behind him.

I exhaled and stepped out from our hiding place. "That was close. Michael, tell me you don't have the flash drive."

"I won't lie," he said. "I have it."

"Why didn't you tell me?"

"There was no time."

"What do you think is stored on it?"

"That's what we're going to find out."

"Here?"

"No. We'll return to the hotel and check it on my laptop. We'll come back here to return the flash drive later."

"Return it? Tonight? Are you serious?"

"We have no choice."

Michael munched on potato chips while he scanned the files he'd loaded on his laptop from Jerry's flash drive. That we'd have to return the flash drive to it original location later grated on my nerves.

In the meantime, I made a pot of coffee from the supplies in our hotel suite. The night was far from over, and I'd need a dose of caffeine to stay awake till after midnight.

I set the mugs on the living room table and sat beside Michael. "Find anything interesting?"

"A whole bunch of names and numbers listed next to them."

Figures ranged from five hundred to several thousand. "Jerry mentioned payoffs when he was speaking on the phone. These numbers could be dollar figures."

Michael reached for his coffee. "That's what I thought. Who would pay Jerry these sums of money and why?"

"Maybe they're cost estimates for each applicant. Jerry said that public funds and government subsidies helped to finance his educational programs."

"If he's running a legitimate operation, why would the information on this flash drive be so hush-hush?"

I ventured a guess. "Maybe he's not reporting it as income."

"Whatever it is, Jerry and his partner in crime are up to something that isn't exactly on the up-and-up."

I wrapped my cold hands around the coffee mug and took a few sips. "It sounds as if Jerry's going to be in serious trouble if he can't find the flash drive."

"Yeah. Whoever he was talking to was threatening him."

"Well then, maybe we shouldn't return it."

Michael smiled. "You know, Megan, you get more devious with each passing day."

"I learned from the best." I poked him in the arm.

He chuckled. "As much as I'd like to pull Jerry's strings, I'll have to play it by the rules. We have to return the flash drive."

"Did you make a copy of the files?"

"You bet." He pulled on his plastic gloves, ejected the flash drive from the laptop, and wiped the prints off it. He checked the time. "It's almost one o'clock. Let's go."

Michael hit the button by the elevator, and we waited for the car to make its ascent to the penthouse.

A sudden loud boom shook the building.

Michael instinctively put his arm around me.

The fire alarm pierced the air, sending a jolt through me. "What was that? A bomb?"

"Whatever it was, we'd better not take the elevator," he said. "Let's take the stairway." He grabbed my hand.

Panic flooded through me as we raced down the stairs. All I kept thinking was *terrorist attack.*

What else but a bomb could have shaken the hotel right up to the tenth floor?

Would another one go off before we exited the building safely?

I tightened my grip on Michael's hand.

The number of guests who joined us in the stairway increased with each lower level we reached. Some people wore jackets and carried knapsacks. Others were dressed in hoodies or jogging outfits. A woman behind me cradled a sleeping baby in a carrier strapped around her shoulders. Faces revealed bewilderment and fear, as if they'd been awakened from their sleep and didn't understand what was happening.

Luckily, the lights were still on, easing the way.

By the time we reached the third floor, our trek down had slowed to a crawl behind other guests. We came to a complete standstill at the second floor.

The fire alarm abruptly stopped.

A wave of chatter mounted as frightened guests expressed their apprehensions.

"It sounded like an explosion," a man wearing bifocals said. "Something definitely set off that alarm. For all we know, it could be a bomb."

The woman with the baby said, "Oh, heavens, no. This can't be happening."

A young couple behind us spoke to each other in French. The woman said something about the high odds of it being a terrorist attack and how they'd experienced a similar incident during a recent visit to England.

Thirty minutes later, we hadn't budged an inch. With so many people packed in the stairway, odors from baby powder to perfume to perspiration meshed in the air.

I couldn't possibly imagine spending the rest of the night camped here. Something had to give.

Michael peeked over the railing. "People are moving forward again."

"Finally." The woman with the baby released an audible sigh. "I can't wait to get out of this hotel." She gazed down at her baby's angelic face.

Such an adorable baby. Too young to die, I thought.

The flow of guests began to trickle downward. As we picked up speed, Michael and I lost sight of the woman with the baby.

We stepped into the lobby and tried to get to the front desk to question the staff, but we could hardly move. Guests from the entire hotel had emptied into the lobby, carting luggage and bearing troubled expressions.

Michael looked at the expansive windows at the front of the hotel. "There's smoke out there. It could be a fire. Let's go see."

A woman standing near us overheard Michael. Having misunderstood him, she said, "You can't go outside. They told us no one is allowed to leave the hotel. We're on lockdown."

32

An explosive device had gone off in a British pub several doors down from the Dorfin Hotel. Details about the blast spread as guests accessed their phones and other electronic devices to find out more about the incident.

People continued to filter into the lobby from the upper floors, their stunned faces assimilating them into the existing throng of apprehensive visitors. They crammed the front desk and sought answers from administrative staff who probably knew as little as the rest of us.

Michael and I edged our way to the windows at the front of the hotel. The scene outside was chaotic.

Municipal law enforcement officers had cordoned off the area with yellow police tape. Their dark uniforms, protective gear, and weapons were reminders that no place was safe from unexpected, horrific incidents in today's world.

Medical teams were tending to the injured.

Firefighters were working to control the blaze.

Police investigators were interviewing witnesses.

Forensic investigators would soon arrive to process the scene—and the victims.

Michael used his phone to access the Internet. Updated news reports indicated five fatalities so far.

In contrast to the upheaval outdoors, hotel staff made their way through the lobby, consoling people and downplaying rumors of a fire in the hotel. Although the impact of the explosion had triggered the hotel's fire alarm system, they claimed no damage had occurred within the building.

Despite staff efforts to convince guests to return to their rooms, the lobby remained packed. Some people preferred to wait their turn to take the elevators rather than climb the stairs. Others wanted to stay in the lobby and close to the main floor exits for a while longer—just in case.

An hour later, the crowds had barely thinned out. Michael suggested we take the stairs back to the penthouse.

On our way to the stairwell, the young woman and her baby fell into stride behind us. I hadn't noticed it earlier, but she was pulling a sizable piece of luggage. She'd probably carried it all the way down the stairs.

I touched Michael's arm. "That woman with the baby..."

I didn't have to say another word.

Michael turned and asked the woman if he could help her with the luggage.

She smiled with relief. "Oh, yes. Thank you."

We made small talk as we climbed the stairs. Sally was a single mother and had given birth to a baby boy four months ago. She'd come to town to visit a friend.

The young mother tried to keep up with us but had to stop at the third floor to catch her breath. "Sorry. I'm a little short-winded."

"That's okay," I said. "I'm a little out of breath too. Let's take a break. There's no rush."

"Thank goodness my baby is still asleep, and it's not time for his feeding yet."

A glimpse at the infant in her arms stirred emotions inside me that only hormones can trigger—a longing to nurture and protect a newborn. The baby photos at the women's clinic had awakened the same feeling.

In the next moment, I brushed those thoughts aside. Having a baby wasn't a commitment I was prepared to make.

~

Nothing could have roused Michael and me from a deep slumber after we'd tumbled into bed at three in the morning. Nothing, that is, except a phone call.

I forced one eye open and checked the clock on the bedside table. "Who would dare call us at eight o'clock on a Sunday morning?"

Michael reached for his phone and answered. "Hi, Agnes... Okay... Right. See you in about an hour." He ended the call. "Agnes asked if we could go over. Something about important developments."

I grabbed a pillow and shouted into it. "No, no, no." My venting over, I sat up. "I'm telling you, Michael, after this trip we're going to need a real vacation."

"No kidding." He stepped out of bed. "I'm going to take a shower."

I admired his sleek muscular body as he moved towards the ensuite. We'd lived together for several years now, yet the sight of him still gave me butterflies.

I wrapped my arms around my knees, my thoughts jolting to the horrific event that had triggered the fire alarm in the hotel last night. The hotel had remained on lockdown, so we'd had to delay our plans to sneak back into Jerry's office to return the flash drive.

My calves ached from climbing those flights of stairs the night before. I massaged them, knowing that I'd feel the pain for days.

I picked up the remote. I'd catch the local news on TV while I waited for my turn in the shower.

As expected, the explosion in the British pub had made the headlines. Police confirmed the perpetrator was a naturalized citizen of Pakistani origin. Witnesses claimed the man had shouted threats in Arabic before detonating the explosives on his suicide vest.

Experts on terrorism were interviewed and gave their opinions on the incident, including their suspicions the perpetrator was a radicalized jihadist. They stated that terrorists typically shout a threat in Arabic because they know it strikes fear in the hearts of non-believers.

A similar incident had occurred in Ottawa several years earlier. A lone gunman—or lone wolf—had shot a soldier on ceremonial sentry duty at the Canadian War Memorial. The perpetrator had subsequently gained access to the Parliament Buildings where he had a shootout with security personnel and was killed. Security on the grounds was beefed up in the aftermath.

The TV broadcast now switched to other news. A police spokesperson stated that the investigation involving Becca Landry was still ongoing, and there was nothing new to report. When questioned by reporters about the recent demise of Frank Landry, the spokesperson issued a similar comment.

Michael came out of the ensuite, a towel wrapped around his hips, his dark hair damp and disheveled. The aroma of fresh pine filled the air. *Too bad we had other plans this morning.*

I cleared my thoughts and briefed him on the news about the explosion. "Why do people have to resort to such brutal ways to get their message across?"

"Tell me about it. I hate to say it, but I think it's only going to get worse."

I hopped out of bed. "Maybe Agnes has good news for us today. I need something positive to lift my spirits after last night. I'll go take a shower now."

His eyes flitted over me in a frisky sort of way. "Yeah, before I forget what we're supposed to be doing this morning."

~

"I have some distressing news to share with you." Agnes eased herself into the armchair while Michael and I sat down on the sofa. "Detective Grist came by yesterday with the preliminary results from Frank's autopsy." She heaved a deep sigh. "My son died from an overdose of fentanyl."

I inhaled sharply. "Oh, Agnes. I'm so sorry."

"Sorry to hear that," Michael said.

Agnes grew teary. "Frank was depressed, and I didn't know how to help him."

I reached over and touched her arm. "Please, don't blame yourself."

"I tried so hard to make it easier for him. For Becca too."

"I'm sure you did."

Agnes blotted her tears with a tissue. "Did I did tell you that Frank had met with the insurance company to sign papers after Becca's death?"

"Regarding her insurance policy?"

"Yes. They called me to say that Frank made arrangements through his lawyer. A trust fund will be set up for the children from the proceeds of Becca's policy."

The notion that Frank had made such arrangements and then killed himself tore at my heart.

Agnes sniffed. "Frank was a good man. Family meant a lot to him. He named me as trustee in his will and left me this house to make sure we'd all be taken care of after he—" Tears flowed freely. She took out another tissue and wiped her eyes. "It's time to move on. I have the children to think of. They need me to be strong for them now."

I simply nodded. I didn't know what to say. The children had lost both parents within days. My attention drifted idly to a cardboard box under the coffee table.

Agnes gestured toward it. "Would you mind sliding that box

over here, Megan? Detective Grist dropped off Becca's things from the office."

I handed it to her.

She pulled out a framed certificate. "This might interest you." She held it out to me.

Michael peered over my right shoulder while I examined it.

Becca's name was written in a fancy script on letter-size paper. The red seal at the bottom of the sheet confirmed she was a graduate of the National Academy of Higher Education. It was probably one of the certificates I'd seen hanging on a wall in her office.

"My memory could be failing me," Agnes said, "but I don't recall Becca ever leaving the house to go take that course."

"Maybe she took a distance learning course," I suggested. "Students can take courses online from practically any location these days."

"That's beside the point. If you examine the date, you'll see that it's dated a year ago."

"Is that significant?"

"Becca started working at Looking Forward a year ago. She never mentioned the course. At the least, Frank would have mentioned it."

Michael and I exchanged side-glances. According to Frank, Becca only had a high school education. Had he lied to us?

Or had Becca chosen not to tell Frank about her advanced learning achievements?

Agnes pulled out another framed certificate. "This one is dated two years ago. Becca never mentioned this course either." She passed it to me.

The script style was the same, as was the red seal affixed to the certificate. The Association of Private Colleges and Schools had issued it. Another name unfamiliar to me. It was yet another indication that Becca had studied beyond her high school days.

I noticed the witness signatures on the certificates and almost gasped aloud. One of them was Lotty Banks!

I coughed to hide my surprise, then brushed a finger over the area covering the signature as if to wipe off a bit of dust.

My subtle action caught Michael's attention. "Agnes, did you talk to the detective about these certificates?"

"No, I didn't because... Well, honestly, I've come to rely on you more." She smiled at us.

"Can we keep them? We'd like to check them out. We'll let you know what we find."

"Of course." She sighed. "Every day brings more questions about Becca. Sometimes I ask myself if we knew her as well as we thought we did." She paused in thought. "Oh, did you find out anything about the rows of signatures on the back of the kids' drawings?"

Michael avoided a direct answer. "We're still looking into it."

"I thought about those signatures as I went through these items from Becca's office." She frowned. "It's all so strange, isn't it? Weird names and mysterious certificates?"

Indeed it was.

A theory began to take shape in my mind—along with a shocking realization that would only complicate our efforts to solve Becca's murder.

33

There was no denying it. Lotty Banks was the same name and witness signature on Becca's certificates as the one repeated multiple times on the back of her children's drawings.

And the same name on the blank certificates with red or gold seals under Jerry's desk.

The bottom line: Becca had signed her own certificates. This fact was the catalyst that triggered more research after our visit with Agnes.

On our return to the hotel, Michael discovered a wealth of information online regarding "diploma or degree mills." These bogus college and university accreditation agencies prospered from the sale of fake educational credentials or diplomas.

I sat on the sofa in our suite and stared at the screen while Michael slowly scrolled down the list of names on his laptop. "Do you believe this stuff, Megan?"

I pointed to the screen. "Those two educational institutions are the same as the ones on Becca's framed certificates."

"Agnes was right. Becca didn't attend those courses. How could she? The institutions on her certificates don't even exist."

"Remember how Frank told us Becca couldn't find a job because she had no higher learning credentials?"

"Yeah, and no office experience either. Makes me question the generosity of Jerry's job offer to her."

"What do you mean?"

"I'd bet Jerry viewed Becca as a vulnerable target. Someone he could convince to play his con game."

Excitement ran through my veins. "Do you realize what we uncovered? A diploma mill. An elaborate Internet fraud scam!"

"We might not be the only ones. Remember that guy from the Anti-Fraud Center who left his business card with Agnes?"

"Leo Gagnon. What would he say if we solved this fraud case for him?" I laughed.

Michael took a more logical approach. "I hate to burst your bubble, but we can't prove anything without physical evidence."

"Of course we can. We have Becca's fake certificates. We have practice sheets with the fake names on them."

"It's not enough."

"Why not?"

"We need to find proof that the scam is far-reaching, that lots more people are implicated at the receiving end."

I remembered a wall lined with similar framed certificates. "I know where you can find more certificates. In Ed Finch's office."

Michael's eyes lit up. "Now you're talking. For all we know, Finch might even be a contributor to Jerry's scheme."

"Let me get this straight. Ed Finch and his team draw in applicants for Jerry Leduc's courses. Jerry's staff designs the courses, and Jerry issues signed certificates to those who pass."

"Right, but there's a catch."

"What?

He grinned. "Every applicant passes."

"But Jerry and his partners receive government subsidies. Doesn't anyone in the government question the end results?"

"Why would they? That's the irony behind this scheme.

Nobody suspects an established organization like Jerry's firm. Let's not forget the authentic-looking certificates they issue to successful applicants too."

"So Jerry and Becca used fake names to cover their tracks," I repeated.

"If it were me, I'd use a different name for each institution."

"To make it harder to trace back to them."

"Right."

I had doubts about Becca's culpability. "Maybe I'm biased, but I have a hard time believing Becca would get involved in a fraud scam of this proportion."

"Look at it this way," Michael said. "She was desperately in need of a job a year ago. It made her a vulnerable target. Maybe Jerry threatened to fire her if she didn't play along."

"She could have applied for another job. Those fancy fake certificates could have fooled anyone."

"Why chance it? A diligent employer could have verified the source and discovered they were fake. Then what? Becca could have landed in jail." He shook his head. "Too risky. Without a recommendation letter from Jerry, she wouldn't have had a chance in hell of getting another job in town anyway."

I had another premise that would explain why Becca had stayed on with Jerry, but I didn't want to jump to conclusions, like Michael often warned. "What's next on the agenda?"

"We'll pay Ed Finch a visit Monday morning," he said. "You can keep him occupied while I take pictures of the certificates."

"Take pictures in plain sight?"

"What other choice do we have?"

"You could let Detective Grist or Leo Gagnon handle it."

"There's no time." Michael shut his laptop. "Besides, I'm sure Jerry isn't working alone. We don't want to scare off his accomplice by sending in the cops."

"Ed Finch could be the mystery man Jerry was speaking with on the phone."

"It's possible."

"What do we do about Jerry's flash drive?"

"Let's wait a couple of days. He might go back to the office this weekend to search for it again."

Something nagged at me. "Even if the evidence we collected points to a scam, we have no way of proving that Jerry and his partners in crime benefitted from it financially."

"That's the tough part," Michael said. "The files on Jerry's flash drive only list names and numbers."

"Jerry could explain them away by saying they represent a point system or some other student performance indicator."

"Right." He grew silent, thinking. "Didn't we overhear Jerry talk about bookkeeping records on the phone that night?"

"The other person said they were 'shoddy.' Maybe Jerry keeps two sets of financial records—a dummy set for official public use and a real but hidden set for his personal records."

"Let's leave it for the anti-fraud agent to handle."

I had the rest of the day to work on my ghostwriting project. I was ready to tour the city to take photos of places and events.

But the weather gods were against me. A thunderstorm rolled in, replete with lightning and hail, putting my plans on hold once again.

I did the next best thing and researched local events online, contacting the organizers for more information when possible. By the end of the day, I'd gathered a handful of generous replies. Several respondents even invited me to personally interview them in the coming days. I thanked them but politely declined, explaining that I was leaving town soon.

I could only imagine their reaction if I'd told them the truth: That Michael and I needed every free moment in the next twenty-four hours to catch a cold-blooded killer.

34

The outright flattery that spewed from Michael's mouth had me rolling my eyes as I listened to his conversation on speakerphone. But despite the overblown rhetoric—or because of it, Michael landed an appointment with Ed Finch of Onward Home early Monday morning.

"Assisting us in promoting our organization through the personal accomplishments of our employees is a splendid idea, Michael." Ed intertwined his bony fingers and smiled at us from across his desk. "How can I help you accomplish that?"

Playing the part with a digital camera hanging from his neck, Michael displayed his usual charm. "If it's okay with you, Ed, I'd like to take photos of your staff to support my article on drug rehab."

"The photos will highlight the professionalism of your staff and workplace," I added.

"Splendid idea," Ed said. "Where would you like to take the photos?"

"In each of the staff offices," Michael said. "I'd like to capture the personal aspect of the services you offer. I promise it won't take long."

"Excellent." Ed stood up. "I'll let my staff know right away. Come with me."

We followed Ed along the corridor and waited while he knocked on each of four office doors. He introduced us, then asked his staff if they could spare a few moments to pose for a photo in their respective offices.

While Michael took photos in the first office, I engaged Ed in conversation. My mission was to distract him from what Michael was actually doing: taking photos of employees beside their framed credentials, then zooming in on their certificates. Whether the documents were authentic or not was something we would determine later.

I stood with Ed in the corridor and away from open office doors while Michael put his strategy into action. "Ed, as you know, I'm helping Michael with research for his article. Can I ask you a few questions?"

"I'd be delighted."

I tapped a few buttons on my phone. "Okay if I record our conversation?"

"Absolutely. I have nothing to hide."

"You mentioned that you work with therapists and other consultants. Tell me how you go about recruiting qualified staff to ensure they're a proper fit with your organization."

"I run an ad and choose from among the best applicants I interview," Ed said.

I subtly looked past him toward the corridor. Michael had moved on to the second office. "Do the applicants need to meet strict criteria?"

"Perhaps strict if we consider the basic job requirements. Some positions are quite demanding."

"What would be examples of those requirements?"

"Let me see." Ed scratched his nose. "Candidates must be honest. I would say competent and dependable too."

"Are employees hired on a trial or probationary period?"

"No. Their résumés speak for themselves."

I caught a glimpse of Michael entering the third office. "Do you verify their academic credentials?"

"It's not necessary," Ed said. "Candidates usually support their applications with letters of reference from indisputable sources."

"So you're saying you don't verify their credentials?"

He blinked. "I can assure you that every case is reviewed according to established protocols."

"Have you ever received complaints from applicants about their dealings with your staff?"

"Never. I run a professional establishment. In fact, candidates often praise my team for the work they do."

"That's good to hear." I was running out of questions.

Ed looked over his shoulder. "Ah, there's Michael now."

"One more to go," Michael said to him, entering the fourth and last office.

Ed took a few steps toward him.

I panicked and called out, "Ed, wait!"

He turned around. "Oh. Sorry, Megan. Did you have more questions?"

"No. I wanted to thank you. It's not every day that we get to meet business people who are so generous with their time."

He let out a squeaky chuckle. "You're welcome. It's not every day that we're offered free publicity."

I had to keep him talking a bit longer. "We'll be sure to send you the finished product."

"I look forward to it." He turned to go.

Just then Michael walked out of the last office and strolled up to us. "All done, except for your office, Ed. May we?"

"Of course." Ed led the way into his office. He raised his chin and puffed out his scrawny chest with pride as he posed in front of the wall displaying his certificates.

Were his certificates forged too?

I was itching to probe further into the photos Michael had taken. Fortunately, he hastily wrapped things up.

"Be sure to let me know when you publish your article," Ed said to him.

"You bet," Michael said as we hurried out.

~

On our return to the hotel, Michael transferred the photos to his laptop. We sat in our usual spots to view them.

My adrenaline surged when I recognized the names of two fake institutions in the framed certificates hanging in one of the staff offices of Onward Home. Others included the University of Renfrew and Ashwood University, both apparently located in Florida. Though their names sounded authentic, they were on the list of fraudulent educational organizations displayed on the Internet.

Worse. The witness signatures on the certificates included Becca's aliases: Lotty Banks and Barbara Lord. The second name on the certificates was a man's and unfamiliar, though we already suspected Jerry Leduc had used other aliases as well when he signed these documents. His choice of surnames could be interpreted as a play on words and had me in giggles: Gerald Duke and Gary Prince.

After we completed our examination, we had enough evidence to prove that Ed Finch and his team of consultants were indeed impostors.

Was his organization merely a link in the chain of widespread fraud we'd uncovered?

How many people had they scammed?

What was the payoff?

We'd get the answers to these questions and more soon enough, but first we needed help from people we could trust with our lives.

35

Michael's call to agent Leo Gagnon of the Anti-Fraud group produced a faster and more positive outcome than we'd anticipated. After Michael explained how our research into fraudulent certificates had turned up evidence that might prove interesting to him, the agent voiced immediate interest and paid us a visit at the hotel.

Leo Gagnon unbuttoned his jacket and leaned his black portfolio against the side of the armchair before sitting down. At his request, Michael removed Becca's certificates from their picture frames so he could examine them more carefully.

Through bifocals balanced on his nose, Leo inspected Becca's certificates with attentiveness. He turned the papers every which way, then placed them on the coffee table. "These are fraudulent certificates. I admit they are excellent copies but fake nonetheless. Whoever designed them was extremely familiar with the process."

"An Internet search revealed the names of the institutions on these papers were fake," I said. "Is there another way to confirm it?"

Leo removed his bifocals. "Not really. An Internet search is fairly reliable. Our group also maintains a list of unaccredited institutions, but it's difficult to keep it up to date because of the fluidity of the perpetrators."

Michael leaned forward. "Fluidity?"

"Yes. Scam artists can easily change the names, websites, and countries where they claim they operate. We can't keep up with all the changes."

"What are the chances of placing criminal charges against scammers?"

"The act of using falsified credentials isn't a specific crime under the Criminal Code in Canada. However, if there's a paper trail, it's a different story."

"How so?"

Leo gestured to the certificates on the table. "For example, we might be able to prove that these fake certificates were obtained and used by an employee to deceive an employer into hiring them. Becca Landry, the recipient of these certificates, might or might not fit into that category. It depends."

"On what?"

"If she believed it was legitimate to receive a degree based on an assessment of life experience or study, she might actually have been a victim."

The pieces of the puzzle were beginning to fall into place. Jerry had offered Becca a job and bogus academic credentials to go with it. No wonder she was afraid to quit her job and search for another one. She didn't want to take the chance that another employer would discover her certificates were phony.

"So you're saying the certificates Becca received were fake, but she could have been totally ignorant about how the system worked," I said.

"That's correct," Leo said. "The certificates she received certainly don't fit into the other category."

"What other category?" Michael asked him.

"Diploma or degree mill operations that sell fake academic credentials from highly regarded universities and institutions."

"What are the differences?"

"Skilled forgers have the ability to crack the watermark. This opens up the potential for forging all kinds of transcripts and creating copies that are identical to the real thing."

"Identical?" I asked. "Like even the weight of paper?"

"Yes," Leo said. "Plus the quality of the paper, the fonts, wording, layout, and other elements. Forgers who operate online are raking it in. All they need is a client's credit card number."

"Sounds like a lucrative business," Michael said.

"That it is," Leo said. "We've uncovered scams that brought in several hundred to several thousand dollars per document, depending on the importance to the client. We've seen everything from fake résumés to fake PhD diplomas. Worldwide, forged degrees are a billion dollar industry."

"People will pay plenty to fast-track online degrees."

"It's nothing new. We have forgeries going back twenty years. The Internet makes it easier for forgers these days."

I had another question. "Doesn't the Internet make it easier for employers to verify academic credentials too?"

Leo nodded. "They have faster access to online resources these days, so they can check their candidates more closely. However, not all employers are thorough. We discovered that the practice of using fake diplomas is still extensive today, ranging from corporate CEOs to federal government positions."

"I bet it's kept under wraps at top levels of government," Michael said. "It could present a high security risk."

"Extremely high security risk," Leo agreed. "If terrorists and other saboteurs use fake credentials to apply for employment in high-ranking jobs, they can gain access to administrative positions in our most sensitive federal departments."

I shuddered at that thought. "Aren't there safeguards to prevent that from happening?"

"The people working in our human resources department contact the degree-granting institution directly to confirm an applicant's credentials," Leo said. "Our staff is very vigilant, but slip-ups can happen."

Michael discreetly introduced the next topic. "On another subject that's connected to Becca Landry, you might have heard that she recently passed away."

"Yes, yes, it was on the news. I thought I recognized the name."

"We're helping the police with their investigation into her death. Detective Grist is handling the case. He'd be interested in hearing what you told us about Becca's certificates."

"You put me in a tough spot." Leo pressed his lips together. "I'm familiar with the investigation. I can say no more about it. However, I'll pass the information along to the detective. Do you have more of these documents?"

"Only in photos I recently took." Michael briefed the agent about our trip to Ed Finch's offices.

"Send them to my email address." Leo handed Michael his business card. "We can pick up a lot from photos too. Anything else?"

"We have these papers." I scooped up the small pile that Agnes had given us. I explained how Becca's different aliases were repeated on the sheets, and how we suspected she and Jerry Leduc had co-signed certificates using different aliases.

Perception glistened in Leo's eyes. "Thank you." He put the papers in his portfolio and stood up. "I'll get our handwriting analyst to take a look at the material. Have a good evening."

After Leo left, Michael and I discussed our next move.

"Should we wait until Leo notifies Detective Grist about the potential criminal evidence we gave him?" I asked him.

He raised his hands in an impatient gesture. "When will that be? Tomorrow? We can't afford to wait even that long."

"So we should contact Detective Grist directly and—"

"We can't do that either. It would trigger an immediate crackdown on Jerry and his scammers."

"Isn't that our end goal?"

"Yes, but the last thing we need is Grist finding out that we have Jerry's flash drive in our possession. He'd charge us with a break-in and theft."

He was dismissing my suggestions at every turn. Something was bothering him. "What's wrong, Michael?"

He ran a hand through his hair. "I think we moved too fast by calling the anti-fraud guy."

"We had no choice. It's a question of time before Jerry gets wise to us—if he hasn't already."

He took a moment to think. "Okay. I'll send an email to Grist, but I'll time it for delivery so that he gets it after we return Jerry's flash drive tonight. First things first."

"Okay. Tonight."

Michael was right. Time was of the essence.

We had to ensure that the police would find the flash drive in its original setting. It was critical evidence that they—not to mention the anti-fraud group—would find extremely useful to their investigation.

But going back to Jerry's office tonight scared the living daylights out of me.

36

At eleven o'clock Monday night, Michael and I entered the premises that housed Looking Forward. It was our last chance to sneak into Jerry's office and drop off the flash drive before his counterfeit scam blew wide open.

We made a dash up the stairwell but tread lightly, checking behind every corner. No one was around.

Using our flashlights and Becca's spare key, we opened the door to Jerry's firm. Nothing had changed in his cluttered office —a sign that he hadn't returned to search for his flash drive.

"I'll leave it exactly where I found it," Michael said. "Behind this table."

All of a sudden, the front door to the office slammed shut.

The overhead lights in the corridor came on.

Michael looked as astounded as I felt.

Footsteps approached.

A male form stopped in the doorway. He flicked the lights on in the office.

It was Jerry. With a gun aimed at us. "Did you really think you'd get away with it?" he sneered.

"I should be asking you the same question," Michael said.

Jerry laughed. "I can get you both arrested for trespassing and theft. You've got nothing on me."

Michael slowly edged in front of me to shield me from Jerry. "We have enough to put you behind bars for a very long time."

Jerry grasped his gun tighter. "Don't take another step."

Michael stopped.

"What did you do with the flash drive you stole from me?"

"I didn't steal your flash drive."

"You're lying. I didn't know how you got into my office, but someone saw you and reported it."

The janitor!

Jerry continued. "Then I remembered no one had returned Becca's keys to the office after she died. Someone else still had them. Someone who was nosy enough to break into my office."

Michael launched one of his diversion techniques. "The cops are onto you, Jerry. They know you killed Becca."

Jerry blinked, seemed dazed. He recovered in the next moment. "You're crazy. You think I don't know you've been snooping around? I have important connections everywhere in the city. They told me how you're trying to dredge up trouble and put me out of business."

"Your connections won't save you from a murder rap. They'll turn their backs on you to save themselves."

"You're all talk," Jerry scoffed. "You can't prove a thing."

"Innocent people died because of you. Including Dylan."

"Who's Dylan?"

"The delivery service attendant at the Dorfin Hotel."

Jerry said nothing.

"Don't pretend you don't know him. He was your go-to guy for street drugs."

Jerry squinted. "Oh, you mean the guy who ran errands for drug addicts? I heard about him on the news. Poor sucker."

Undeterred, Michael pressed on. "You used him to get the liquid fentanyl that killed Becca."

I stifled a gasp.

Michael was guessing.

But would Jerry buy it?

"You're trying every trick in the book to pin her death on me, aren't you?" Jerry snickered. "Go ahead. Prove it."

Inspired by Michael's bravado, I moved forward. "Jerry, you threatened Becca and forced her to sign fake certificates or else you'd fire her. You paid her a load of money to keep her from quitting her job—like two thousand dollars in cash the Friday she died."

Jerry smirked. "You're wrong. I gave that little tramp a chance to make a decent living. I rescued her from a life in the gutter so she could be a proper wife and mother."

His revelation stunned me.

Jerry feigned sadness. "Oh, so sorry to have shocked you, Megan."

I gathered my composure. "So you already knew Becca."

"And how! I first met her in her previous life as an escort before she cleaned up her act and married that military guy. She was trouble even back then. She called the cops on me after our dinner date because I refused to pay the bill. Hell, I'd already paid plenty for the room."

Becca's cheap dinner date! It was Jerry!

Jerry went on. "Sure, she'd changed her appearance since the good old days, but I recognized her all the same. She didn't remember me, but so what? The fact I knew her intimately made it that much easier to gain her loyalty. If you know what I mean." He ogled me.

My disgust for him increased with each passing moment. "What about the money in Becca's purse?"

"It was legit. I paid her salary in cash and threw in a bonus for the overtime hours she'd worked."

"That's a lie," I shouted. "That money was a bribe. You argued with Becca the Friday afternoon she walked out of here because she threatened to expose your counterfeit scam to the police. She wanted to quit her job. She didn't want to play your sick little game anymore."

Jerry blinked. "Becca was lazy. I had to shake some common sense into her a couple of times."

"Shake? How?"

"I'd grab her and shake her." He pumped his hands in the air.

That explained the bruises on Becca's arms!

I took a step forward. "You miserable, vindictive—"

Michael grabbed my arm and held me back.

Jerry raised his voice. "Hey! If anyone was a victim, it was me. We had a deal—fentanyl pills in exchange for a few lousy signatures."

Another bombshell admission. Jerry was Becca's supplier!

"She got greedy. She wanted more money—lots more. She threatened to blackmail me if I didn't pay up."

"Another lie! You gave her two thousand dollars to stay on and keep quiet about your scam. But you didn't trust her, so you killed her."

Jerry forced a smile. "You'd better make nice with me, Megan. If you don't, I'll make sure you—"

"You won't put a finger on her." Michael eyed him with the ferocity of a jungle cat. "Or I'll tear you apart with my bare hands."

Though Jerry had a marked advantage over us, his hand trembled slightly. "You're forgetting whose office you broke into. One phone call to the police and—"

"Go ahead," Michael said. "Make the call. Your time is up anyway. We traced the names on your certificates to a bunch of fake academic institutions. Your witness signatures—all aliases —are on them. Becca's aliases too."

Jerry glared at him and repeated his comeback. "Prove it."

"We did. We thought the police and the anti-fraud guys would be interested in your rip-off scheme too. So we sent them the evidence we collected."

"You're bluffing."

"Try me." Michael folded his arms. "Call Grist and ask him."

"Both of you, it's time to go," Jerry snarled, motioning with his gun toward the door. "I don't want to shoot you here and dirty my office."

Michael stood his ground. "We're not going anywhere."

"Oh, but you definitely are." A deep voice boomed from the corridor.

Randall Thorne appeared in the doorway, aiming his gun at Michael and me.

37

"You think you know everything about me, don't you?" Jerry mocked Michael. "Randall is proof that my connections are high up in the echelon. These people have my back."

"Not for long," Michael said.

"I'm disappointed in you, Michael," Randall said, his deep voice resonating with more threatening emotions. "You told me you came to town to cover more significant matters."

Michael shrugged. "What can I say? I got sidetracked. Finding a dead body in my hotel room does that to me." He paused. "Sorry. *Your* hotel room."

Randall switched his gaze to me. "Megan, surely you're not usually involved in such lurid affairs. An attractive woman like you should be showered with the finer things in life."

Anger boiled inside me. "The way you showered Becca? Conspiring with Jerry to make sure she got a keycard to your hotel room that weekend. Ordering room service for Becca so Jerry could drop liquid fentanyl into the wine before it was delivered."

Jerry's lips quivered. He shot an anxious glance at Randall. "How did—"

"Don't listen to this drivel," Randall retorted.

"Jerry, your partner devised the perfect scam and cheated the government out of millions of dollars," Michael said. "I know it wasn't your idea. You don't have the expertise—or the brains—to dream up such an elaborate scheme."

"You're all mouth, you know that?" Jerry shifted from one foot to the other, as if he were about to pounce on Michael.

"Cool down, Jerry," Randall said, then addressed Michael and me. "Thanks to our business connections, thousands of applicants have certificates from educational institutions and a better chance of getting a job."

"Yeah, educational institutions that exist only in the virtual world," Michael said. "Wait till your employers do background checks."

"If you're referring to government sponsors, they won't bother with such trivialities," Randall said. "They don't have the time or the resources. It might interest you that we haven't heard a peep from private employers either."

"Most of your applicants are still unemployed, that's why."

Jerry cut in, repeating his buzzword. "Prove it."

Michael egged him on. "Randall is using you, Jerry. You're no better than a doormat to him. Want to know why he got Ed Finch involved in the scam as a go-between? Because he's a lot more capable than you are."

Jerry snorted. "That's not true. We're equal partners." He waited, expecting confirmation from Randall, but the man remained stone-faced.

Michael persisted in provoking Jerry. "Randall let you handle the bookkeeping aspects of the scam instead. A simple job for a simple mind, but you bungled that up big time."

"You don't know what the hell you're talking about." Jerry nervously looked at Randall who showed no reaction.

"We found evidence of applicant names and thousands of dollars you received in payoffs." Michael tsk-tsked and wagged a finger at Jerry. "You should have been more careful."

Ripples crossed Randall's forehead, but he remained silent.

"I covered my tracks," Jerry blurted, his eyes twitching before they settled on Randall. "There's no way they could have found out."

Randall glared at him. "Shut up, you fool! Did you get their phones?"

"No. I forgot."

"Then do it."

Jerry rushed up to me, holding out his free hand.

I reached into my handbag and gave him my phone.

Michael was relentless. "Randall is taking you for a sucker, Jerry. Man up to him. Show him what you're worth."

Jerry shoved him against the desk. "Shut up and give me your phone."

Michael handed it over.

With two guns aimed at our backs, we began the slow procession out of the office and into the outer hallway.

Desperate, I looked around for the janitor. There was no sign of him. Damn!

"We'll take the stairs to the underground parking," Randall said.

Jerry led the way down the stairway with Randall at the rear.

My heart hammered in my chest. We needed a distraction —something that would slow down their evil plan.

I pretended to trip on the last stair before the second floor landing. My handbag broke my fall, but I cried out in pain, hoping someone else would hear.

"Keep her quiet," Randall hissed at Michael. "Or I will."

As Michael leaned over me, I winked at him.

He winked back, then helped me to my feet.

"Ouch!" I hung onto his arm, feigning pain. "I think I sprained my ankle."

"She won't be able to walk," Michael said to the other men.

"I don't give a damn. Get going!" Randall's voice was gruff.

Michael wrapped his arm around my waist and helped me down the stairs.

I kept wishing we'd bump into someone on our way down. Then again, who in their right mind would be hanging around an office building after midnight?

When Jerry opened the door to the underground parking, my hopes were dashed. I did a quick count of the vehicles. Three cars and two small white vans leased by individuals or businesses in the building had probably been parked here overnight.

Michael was observing the parked vehicles too as we moved past them.

Panic seized me as the inescapable future became clearer by the second. These two lunatics planned to kill us!

Jerry's fast pace had outdone ours. He turned now and waved us over to the far end of the lot. "This way."

Our footsteps echoed in the vast emptiness of concrete pillars and metal ducts. Dankness filled the air where only these cold, hard structures stood unmoving.

I shivered. If only we'd come here earlier this evening, there might have been more people around. Not that it made any difference at this point.

I hobbled along the oil-stained concrete, stretching time as much as I could. Michael continued to play along with me.

It wasn't as if I expected the cavalry to ride in and save us in the next moment. Rather, I was trying my best to delay the inevitable—our deaths.

Jerry stopped in front of a black Lincoln Town Car parked in the shadows along the back wall. Was it his car?

I hadn't noticed it earlier—partly because of its color and partly because I'd already begun to panic.

"Move!" Randall ordered from behind us.

With only a short distance to go, the space toward our fatal destiny narrowed as Michael and I neared the car.

My heart thumped so hard, I was certain my chest would

burst. I thought of my mother back home in Montreal, my other relatives and friends... Would I ever see them again?

Michael stared at Jerry with apprehension as he tightened his hold around me.

In spite of his supportive grasp, I trembled uncontrollably. Humidity had penetrated my body, but it was nothing compared to the anxiety mounting inside me.

My breathing quickened and I felt woozy.

Would Michael and I spend our last precious moments together in this decrepit underground parking lot?

Or were these goons going to take us elsewhere to carry out their deadly deed?

38

Randall approached the Lincoln Town Car. He looked at Michael and me and waved his gun toward the back seat. "Get in."

Michael held me tighter. "Not a chance."

Randall's voice boomed in the underground cavity. "Get in, or I'll shoot you right here and now!"

Michael didn't budge.

I didn't know what game Michael was playing, but something told me Randall would have no qualms in cutting short our lives. The photo we'd seen in Jerry's office implied he was familiar with handling guns.

Jerry approached the driver's side of the car, his gun no longer pointing at us. He cast a worried look toward Randall before getting behind the wheel.

Randall's voice was less certain than it had been moments earlier. "I'm warning you. Get in or else." He stretched his arm out and aimed the gun at us.

Bright lights burst on all sides.

Car doors opened.

Feet scuffled.

A man's voice called out, "Police! Drop your weapons!"

"Run!" Michael grabbed my arm and we scrambled away.

A cacophony of gunshots resounded behind us, ricocheting against concrete pillars, pinging into metal ducts and pipes.

Michael shoved me behind a pillar and shielded me with his body.

More shots rang out, echoing in the almost empty space.

A vehicle roared to life, then another.

Car doors slammed shut and tires squealed.

Jerry's car sped by our hiding spot. The windows were tinted, so I couldn't see if Randall was inside the car or not.

A white van zoomed past, its tires spraying dust in the air.

I could feel Michael's heart pounding as I rested my head against his chest. Terror filled me and I shut my eyes, praying for this horrendous scene to stop.

"They can't make it out of here," Michael said. "The exterior door won't lift fast enough."

Tires screeched.

Metal crashed into metal.

A car horn blared.

"Get out of the vehicle with your hands over your head!" The same voice I'd heard earlier told me the police had won this round.

"I'm hurt," Jerry hollered. "You shot me!"

The massive garage door lifted with a creak. Two cars sped inside.

Michael stole a glimpse. "It's over," he said to me, his voice soft. "Two cruisers just arrived."

I inhaled deeply, only now aware that I'd been holding my breath for the longest time. The tension in my body began to dissipate.

Michael slowly moved away from me, his hands in the air.

"Michael? What's wrong?"

I heard a distinctive sound behind us: the cocking of a gun.

Randall was pointing his gun at us.

My heart picked up speed. I started to shake.

In an eerily quiet voice, Randall said to Michael, "Move back real slow, or I'll blow your head open."

Michael took a few steps back.

"Where's your car?" Randall asked.

"On a side street," Michael said.

Randall grabbed my arm and yanked me toward him. "You're my ticket out of here." He held the gun to my temple. "Let's go for a walk. Michael, you first."

Michael kept his hands raised as we advanced at a slow and steady pace across the parking lot. Chances were that the police would see him and not take a shot in our direction.

Up ahead, two police cruisers and a white van had surrounded Jerry's car. The van had cut off his escape, resulting in a smashed hood to Jerry's car.

Jerry was sitting in the driver's seat, his head buried in the inflated airbag, his car horn blaring. Two police officers pulled him out. While one of them turned off the car horn, the other escorted Jerry to a cruiser and ushered him into the back seat.

Randall prodded us along the shadowy borders of the lot. If he assumed we'd succeeded in making it out of the parking area, he'd have to think twice about the obstacles ahead—the squadron of police officers and their vehicles.

Four officers stood next to a man in plainclothes who gestured toward the lot and appeared to be giving them orders. He noticed us and swiftly drew his gun. "Stop! Hold it right there!"

It was Detective Grist!

The other officers instantly drew their weapons and aimed them in our direction.

The detective reinforced his warning. "Stop or we'll shoot!"

"Not if you want me to shoot this couple first," Randall shouted back. He tugged on my arm, pulling me in front of him as a shield. All the while, he kept his gun pressed to my head.

I was a hostage with no viable options for escape. My knees

felt wobbly. I wasn't sure I'd be able to walk up the incline that led out of the parking lot.

The officers kept their guns aimed at us. How could they possibly disarm Randall and not shoot Michael or me in the process?

Would one of them actually take a chance and shoot?

What were the chances that Michael and I wouldn't be hurt —or even die—from stray bullets?

Slim to none.

An ambulance siren wailed in the distance. Was it on its way here?

Detective Grist gave Michael a subtle hand signal. It was so subtle that I wondered if I hadn't imagined it.

Michael showed no response. The moment had passed.

Randall's breathing was forced, and the pressure of his gun against my head was unsteady.

What if he slipped and fell? Would he accidentally discharge his gun and kill me?

Don't panic, I told myself. Try to calm down. You'll think more clearly.

Our party of three edged past the police squad positioned to the left of us.

Unmoving, the officers kept their weapons aimed in our direction. Would one of them shoot at the first opportune moment?

Trigger fingers could slip. Eyes could misread the situation. There was no room for error.

My pulse raced. So much for trying to calm down.

As we climbed the incline that led to the street, Randall's pace slackened. He was getting tired.

I stole a glimpse at Michael. He was slowing down too. For someone who jogged and worked out in the gym almost every day, climbing this slight slope shouldn't be a difficult feat for him.

But Randall wouldn't know that.

I took Michael's cue and took smaller steps, reducing my pace.

Randall noticed. He yanked me forward, switching his attention from the police to the open entryway.

The ambulance siren was getting louder now. It had to be heading in our direction!

As we inched up the slope to the open entryway, Michael slackened his pace even more. He gradually fell behind us.

I didn't dare sneak a peek at Randall. I had to assume he was too busy watching the police to notice that Michael was no longer in front of us.

The barrel of Randall's gun had slid down during our climb and was now level with my neck. Randall hadn't noticed this either. If only I could break away…

The siren blared at full blast as the ambulance flew in through the open entrance. It was coming right at us!

Randall flinched, loosening his grasp on my arm.

I broke away and darted to the right. I prayed Randall's reflex would be slow and his aim lousy.

The ambulance came to a screeching halt.

Randall shrieked like a wild animal.

I turned, expecting to see him pinned under the ambulance.

But no. Michael had him in a chokehold!

Randall's arms flailed and he fired a shot.

The paramedics inside the vehicle ducked for cover.

The bullet had lodged in the front hood of the ambulance, narrowly missing the windshield.

Police officers jumped into the melee, struggling to hold Randall down while they retrieved his gun and Detective Grist handcuffed him.

"I demand to call my lawyer," Randall shouted as officers escorted him to the other cruiser.

Michael rushed up to me, wrapped his arms around me. "Megan, are you okay?"

"Y-yes." I was shaking, trying to catch my breath. "And you?"

"I'm good." He held me closer. "I thought I was going to lose you, Megan."

My eyes filled with happy tears. "You're my hero, you know that?"

The sound of a car engine broke into the moment.

A police cruiser drove off with Randall in tow. Two other officers accompanied Jerry to the ambulance. He was able to walk but was holding his left arm. The front of his shirt was seeped in blood.

Detective Grist strode up to Michael and me. "You both okay?"

"Nothing that a good night's rest can't fix." Michael kept a protective arm around me.

Concern tightened the detective's expression. "I'm sorry you had to go through this, Michael. When you sent me the email earlier, I didn't expect you'd offer yourself and Megan up as bait for Randall Thorne."

"Believe me, it wasn't supposed to play out like this. How did you know to come here?"

"The same names kept coming up in our investigation into Becca Landry's death. Jerry Leduc and Randall Thorne, among others. When Leo Gagnon of the Anti-Fraud group contacted me and inquired about them, I realized it wasn't a fluke."

"How did you know Jerry and Randall would be here?" I asked the detective.

"Your discussion with Leo Gagnon filled in some of the gaps in our investigation. We suspected Thorne might try to leave the country, so we knew we had to move quickly. We requested a trace on his cell phone and followed him here. When the four of you walked into this parking lot, we knew we had trouble on our hands. We didn't expect to confront those two guys in a shootout with you as their hostages." He paused. "How did you end up here anyway?"

"Long story," Michael said. "Let's just say we walked into a trap."

"And we couldn't have been happier to see you," I said to the detective. "Thank you."

"Oh, don't thank me," Detective Grist said. "Thank Michael. We were running out of options to keep you both safe until he jumped into action." He smiled and gave Michael a pat on the back. "I'm glad you caught my hand signal. Just like old times, eh?"

Michael chuckled. "How could I forget? It was one of the best tactics I learned from those takedowns with your Toronto team."

The detective studied us. "You feel like coming to the station now to give me your statements? Your memory might not be as sharp tomorrow morning."

Michael asked, "Megan, do you want to do this now?"

"Absolutely," I said. "For Becca's sake."

39

D etective Grist contacted us over the following weeks in preparation for our court date on the witness stand.

Becca's Landry's murder case against Jerry Leduc and Randall Thorne was progressing well, the detective said, as was the now infamous certificate fraud case. Our testimony would help to solidify the prosecution's case against both men who also faced attempted murder charges in relation to Michael and me.

As news of the arrests hit the media, shock waves rattled the highest echelons of federal bureaucracy. Government administrators and affiliated agencies tripped over themselves to plug leaks that might further blemish the reputation of the political party in power.

As part of his court testimony, Detective Grist disclosed evidence that had surfaced during his investigation into Becca's death. My interest grew when he revealed that he'd accessed Becca's computer with the help of Jerry's office technician.

Becca had recorded conversations on her cell phone and transferred them to a hidden file on her computer. The replay of her office conversation with Jerry that last Friday proved he had threatened her after she insisted she no longer wanted to take part in his fake certificate scheme. When Jerry refused to let her go, she said she was going to report him to the police.

More evidence came to light in court when the detective submitted recordings of phone conversations between Jerry and Randall that the police had seized. The men had developed a last-minute plan to get rid of Becca that same Friday, with Randall requesting service delivery of a carafe of wine and two glasses to room 634.

The defense attorney attempted to show that Jerry wasn't involved in drugging the wine delivered to Becca's hotel room. But a surprise testimony from a guest at the hotel confirmed that an exchange had indeed taken place between Dylan and Jerry in the elevator that Friday afternoon.

The witness to that fatal exchange? None other than Roger. Standing at the back of the elevator, he'd seen Dylan hand Jerry a vial in a small plastic bag but had no idea what it was at the time. A police search in hotel garbage bags produced the vial.

Although the detective had no evidence to implicate Ed Finch in Becca's murder, he didn't escape unscathed. Testimony from Jerry and Randall fingered Ed as a willing partner in their certificates scam. The scheme was Randall's creation, but Ed had carried out the plan by recruiting course applicants from the ranks of students, professionals, immigrants, and drug addicts. His employees were also involved in the scam and charged accordingly.

The fraudulent certificate scheme had come to fruition through Jerry's staff—a composite of real and fictitious course developers. Paying customers received a unique code so they could access the fast-track courses available on the firm's website. The code was Jerry's foolproof way of collecting funds from applicants while barring outsiders.

Applicants ran the spectrum from shrewd consumers who purchased the services with intent to defraud, to naïve buyers who were unaware of the misleading aspect of the services.

Desperate applicants wanting to improve their lives had maxed out credit cards and taken out loans to pay for fake academic diplomas. Angry and disillusioned witnesses came forward in court, eager to share their experiences.

Testimony also disclosed the preparation of fake résumés and letters of reference. It came as no surprise that remarks on the witness stand were heated and accusatory.

An embarrassing revelation that emerged in court implied that government departments and associated agencies had exercised limited oversight. As a consequence, Randall and his partners had succeeded in collecting millions of dollars from government subsidies and private sponsors for more than a decade.

To add to the embarrassment of bureaucratic fat cats whom Randall had wined and dined in exchange for sponsorships, it came to light that many had enjoyed "free keycard" weekends in room 634—escorts included.

Hundreds of Jerry's course "graduates" had been hired by government agencies and associated groups. As expected, these employees feared the loss of their jobs or faced legal battles for misrepresenting themselves to employers by submitting fake credentials.

One case allegedly involved a man who worked for a government agency. He was identified as an illegal immigrant from Morocco. Like many others, he was unwittingly hired based on forged academic credentials issued by Jerry's firm. An unnamed government source informed the media that the employee had leanings toward radicalized terrorism.

The Prime Minister's Office hastily issued a statement to the effect that the government did not condone the criminal actions of such individuals and that, if caught, they would be punished to the full extent of the law. However, no reference was made to the employee alleged to have terrorist leanings. Subsequent attempts by the media to obtain a comment from a government agency spokesperson were rebuffed.

As Tasha would have said, so much for "bureaucratized ambiguity."

In a related investigation, Leo Gagnon of the Anti-Fraud Center revealed that the government was pursuing Jerry, Randall, and Ed in matters of financial fraud and income tax evasion.

Despite the recent turmoil, I wanted to believe in happy endings. So I chose to believe that Becca had planned to talk to Frank at the hotel and get his advice regarding Jerry's threats and her job dilemma. She loved her family and wanted to share the good news about her pregnancy with Frank too. It would have been a new start for both of them.

As I sipped my coffee in our Montreal condo, I watched Michael tap away on his laptop. The first two installments of his investigation covering the illegal fentanyl crisis had gained praise at *The Gazette*. Management eagerly awaited the next installment, which he expected to wrap up soon.

As for my ghostwriting project...

One of the last things on my to-do list before Michael and I had left Ottawa was to contact Tasha. She was ecstatic when I'd told her about the developments in Becca's murder case. She showed her appreciation by giving me photos celebrating the city's 150th anniversary and other photos of historic sites in and around town.

I'd welcomed the return to my humdrum routine and the seclusion of my home office. It provided the respite I needed from our terrifying experience in Ottawa. After I'd submitted my ghostwriting project, my client was so pleased that she gave me another project. This one was based in Montreal.

Home sweet home.

ACKNOWLEDGMENTS

Writing can be a lonely profession, but the support I receive from a dedicated team ensures that I'm never alone. For their skillful input and generosity, I'd like to thank my cover designer, editors, and proofreaders. I also want to thank my family and friends for encouraging me along the path to realizing my dream.

A very special thanks to my readers who inspire me to keep on writing.

ABOUT THE AUTHOR

Sandra Nikolai is the author of the Megan Scott/Michael Elliott Mystery series. In addition to her novels, Sandra has published a string of short crime stories, garnering awards along the way.

A graduate of McGill University in Montreal, Sandra held jobs in sales, finance, and high tech before leaving the corporate world to pursue a career in writing. She likes to think that plotting a whodunit reveals the lighter—yet more mysterious—side of her persona.

Visit Sandra's website at sandranikolai.com to sign up for her exclusive quarterly newsletter and receive free chapters from her books. Your email address will never be shared and you can unsubscribe at any time. Become a fan on Goodreads or Facebook, or follow Sandra on Twitter @SandraNikolai

BOOKS BY SANDRA NIKOLAI

Megan Scott/Michael Elliott Mystery series:

False Impressions

Fatal Whispers

Icy Silence

Dark Deeds

Broken Trust

Cold Revenge